W9-AEE-872

AN IMPERATIVE DUTY.

I.

OLNEY got back to Boston about the middle of July, and found himself in the social solitude which the summer makes more noticeable in that city than in any other. The business, the hard work of life, was going on, galloping on, as it always does in America, but the pleasure of life, which he used to be part of as a younger man, was taking a rest, or if not a rest, then certainly an outing at the sea-shore. He met no one he knew, and he continued his foreign travels in his native place, after an absence so long that it made everything once so familiar bewilderingly strange.

He had sailed ten days before from Liverpool, but he felt as if he had been voyaging in a vicious circle when he landed, and had arrived in Liverpool again. In several humiliating little ways, Boston recalled the most commonplace of English cities. It was not like Liverpool in a certain civic grandiosity, a sort of lion-and-unicorn spectacularity which he had observed there. The resemblance appeared to him in the meanness and dulness of many of the streets in the older part of the town where he was lodged, and in the littleness of the houses. Then there was a curious similarity in the figures and faces of the crowd. He had been struck by the almost American look of the poorer class in Liverpool, and in Boston he was struck by its English look. He could half account for this by the fact that the average face and figure one meets in Boston in midsummer, is hardly American; but the other half of the puzzle remained. He could only conjecture an approach from all directions to a common type among those who work with their hands for a living; what he had seen in Liverpool and now saw in Boston was not the English type or the American type, but the proletarian type. He noticed it especially in the women, and more especially in the young girls, as he met them in the street after their day's work was done, and on the first Sunday afternoon following his arrival, as he saw them in the Common. By far the greater part of those listening to the brass band which was then beginning to vex the ghost of our poor old Puritan Sabbath there, were given away by their accent for those primary and secondary Irish who abound with us. The old women were strong, sturdy, old-world peasants, but the young girls were thin and crooked, with pale, pasty complexions, and an effect of physical delicacy from their hard work and hard conditions, which might later be physical refinement. They were conjecturably out of box factories and clothier's shops; they went about in threes or fours, with their lank arms round one another's waists, or lounged upon the dry grass; and they seemed fond of wearing red jerseys, which accented every fact of their anatomy. Looking at them scientifically, Olney thought that if they survived to be mothers they might give us, with better conditions, a race as hale and handsome as the elder American race; but the transition from the Old World to the New, as represented in them, was painful. Their voices were at once coarse and weak; their walk was uncertain, now awkward and now graceful, an undeveloped gait; he found their bearing apt to be aggressive, as if from a wish to ascertain the full limits of their social freedom, rather than from ill-nature, or that bad-heartedness which most rudeness comes from.

But, in fact, Olney met nowhere the deference from beneath that his long sojourn in Europe had accustomed him to consider politeness. He was used in all public places with a kindness mixed with roughness, which is probably the real republican manner; the manner of Florence before the Medici; the manner of Venice when the Florentines were wounded by it after the Medici corrupted them; the manner of the French when the Terror had done its work. Nobody proved unamiable, though everybody seemed so at first; not even the waiters at his hotel, where he was served by adoptive citizens who looked so much like brigands that he could not help expecting to be carried off and held somewhere for ransom when he first came into the dining-room. They wore immense black mustaches or huge whiskers, or else the American beard cut slanting from the corners of the mouth. They

had a kind of short sack of alpaca, [which did not support one's love of gentility like the conventional dress-
coat of the world-wide waiter,] or cheer one's heart like
the white linen jacket and apron of the negro waiter.
But Olney found them, upon what might be called
personal acquaintance, neither uncivil nor unkind,
though they were awkward and rather stupid. They
could not hide their eagerness for fees, and they took
an interest in his well-being so openly mercenary, that
he could scarcely enjoy his meals. With two of those
four-winged whirligigs revolving on the table before
him to scare away the flies, and working him up to
such a vertigo that he thought he must swoon into his
soup, Olney was uncomfortably aware of the Irish
waiter standing so close behind his chair that his
stomach bulged against it, and he felt his breath coming and going on the bald spot on his crown. He
could not put out his hand to take up a bit of bread
without having a hairy paw thrust forward to antici-
pate his want; and he knew that his waiter considered
each service of the kind worth a good deal extra, and
expected to be remembered for it in our silver coin-
age, whose unique ugliness struck Olney afresh.

He would not have been ready to say that one of
the negro waiters, whom he wished they had at his
hotel, would not have been just as greedy of money;
but he would have clothed his greed in such a smiling
courtesy and such a childish simple-heartedness that it
would have been graceful and winning. He would
have used tact in his ministrations; he would not have

cumbered him with service, as from a wheelbarrow,
but would have given him a touch of help here, and a
little morsel of attention there; he would have kept
aloof as well as alert. That is, he would have had all
these charms if he were at his best, and he would have
had some of them if he were at his worst.

In fact, the one aspect of our mixed humanity here
which struck Olney as altogether agreeable in getting
home was that of the race which vexes our social
question with its servile past, and promises to keep it
uncomfortable with its civic future. He had not forgotten that, so far as society in the society sense is
concerned, we have always frankly simplified the matter, and no more consort with the negroes than we do
with the lower animals, so that one would be quite as
likely to meet a cow or a horse in an American drawing-room as a person of color. But he had forgotten
how entirely the colored people keep to themselves in
all public places, and how, with the same civil rights
as ourselves, they have their own neighborhoods, their
own churches, their own amusements, their own re-
sorts. They were just as free to come to the music
on the Common that Sunday afternoon as any of the
white people he saw there. They could have walked
up and down, they could have lounged upon the grass,
and no one would have molested them, though the
whites would have kept apart from them. But he
found very few of them there. It was not till he followed a group away from the Common through
Charles Street, where they have their principal church,

into Cambridge Street, which is their chief promenade, that he began to see many of them. In the humbler side-hill streets, and in the alleys branching upward from either thoroughfare, they have their homes, and here he encountered them of all ages and sexes. It seemed to him that they had increased since he was last in Boston beyond the ratio of nature; and the hotel clerk afterward told him there had been that summer an unusual influx of negroes from the South.

He would not have known the new arrivals by anything in their looks or bearing. Their environment had made as little impression on the older inhabitants, or the natives, as Time himself makes upon persons of their race, and Olney fancied that Boston did not characterize their manner, as it does that of almost every other sort of aliens. They all alike seemed shining with good-nature and good-will, and the desire of peace on earth. Their barbaric taste in color, when it flamed out in a crimson necktie or a scarlet jersey, or when it subdued itself to a sable that left no gleam of white about them but a point or rim of shirt collar, was invariably delightful to him; but he had to own that their younger people were often dressed with an innate feeling for style. Some of the young fellows were very effective dandies of the type we were then beginning to call dude, and were marked by an ultra correctness, if there is any such thing; they had that air of being clothed through and through, as to the immortal spirit as well as the perishable body, by their cloth gaiters, their light trousers, their neatly-buttoned cutaway coats, their harmonious scarfs, and their silk hats. They carried on flirtations of the eye with the young colored girls they met, or when they were walking with them they paid them a court which was far above the behavior of the common young white fellows with the girls of their class in refinement and delicacy. The negroes, if they wished to imitate the manners of our race, wished to imitate the manners of the best among us; they wished to be like ladies and gentlemen. But the young white girls and their fellows whom Olney saw during the evening in possession of most of the benches in the Common and the Public Garden, and between the lawns of Commonwealth Avenue, apparently did not wish to be like ladies and gentlemen in their behavior. The fellow in each case had his arm about the girl's waist, and she had her head at times upon his shoulder; if the branch of a tree overhead cast the smallest rag or tatter of shadow upon them, she had her head on his shoulder most of the time. Olney was rather abashed when he passed close to one of these couples, but they seemed to suffer no embarrassment. They had apparently no concealments to make, nothing to be ashamed of; and they had really nothing to give them a sense of guilt. They were simply vulgar young people, who were publicly abusing the freedom our civilization gives their youth, without knowing any better, or meaning any worse. Olney knew this, but he could not help remarking to the advantage of the negroes, that among all these couples on the benches

of the Common and the Garden and the Avenue, he
never found a colored couple. He thought that some
of the young colored girls, as he met them walking
with their decorous beaux, were very pretty in their
way. They had very thin, high, piping voices, that
had an effect both of gentleness and gentility. With
their brilliant complexions of lustrous black, or rich
café au lait, or creamy white, they gave a vividness to
the public spectacle which it would not otherwise have
had, and the sight of these negroes in Boston somehow brought back to Olney's homesick heart a sense
of Italy, where he had never seen one of their race.

II.

OLNEY was very homesick for Italy that Sunday night. After two days in Boston, mostly spent in exploring the once familiar places in it, and discovering the new and strange ones, he hardly knew which made him feel more hopelessly alien. He had been five years away, and he perceived that the effort to repatriate himself must involve wounds as sore as those of the first days of exile. The tissues then lacerated must bleed again before his life could be reunited with the stock from which it had been torn. He felt himself unable to bear the pain; and he found no attraction of novelty in the future before him. He knew the Boston of his coming years too well to have any illusions about it; and he had known too many other places to have kept the provincial superstitions of his nonage and his earlier manhood concerning its primacy. He believed he should succeed, but that it would be in a minor city, after a struggle with competitors who would be just, and who might be generous, but who would be able, thoroughly equipped, and perfectly disciplined. The fight would be long, even if it were victorious; its prizes would be hard to win, however splendid. Neither the fight nor the prizes seemed so attractive now as they had seemed at a distance. He

wished he had been content to stay in Florence, where
he could have had the field to himself, if the harvest
could never have been so rich. But he understood,
even while he called himself a fool for coming home,
that he could not have been content to stay without
first coming away.

When he went abroad to study, he had a good deal
of money, and the income from it was enough for him
to live handsomely on anywhere; in Italy it was
enough to live superbly on.   But the friend with
whom he left his affairs, had put all of Olney's eggs
into one basket.   It was the Union Pacific basket
which he chose, because nearly every one in Boston
was choosing it at the same time, with the fatuous
faith of Bostonians in their stocks.   Suddenly Olney's
income dropped from five or six thousand a year to
nothing at all a year; and his pretty scheme of re-
maining in Italy and growing up with the country in
a practice among the nervous Americans who came
increasingly abroad every year, had to be abandoned,
or at least it seemed so at the time.   Now he wished
he had sold some of his depreciated stock, which everybody said would be worth as much as ever some day,
and taken the money to live on till he could begin
earning some.   This was what Garofalo, his friend and
fellow-student in Vienna, and now Professor of the
Superior Studies at Florence, urged him to do; and
the notion pleased him, but could not persuade him. It
was useless for Garofalo to argue that he would have
to get the means of living in Boston in some such

way, if he went home to establish himself ; Olney believed that he should begin earning money in larger sums if not sooner at home. Besides, he recurred to that vague ideal of duty which all virtuous Americans have, and he felt that he ought, as an American, to live in America. He had been quite willing to think of living in Italy while he had the means, but as soon as he had no means, his dormant sense of patriotism roused itself. He said that if he had to make a fight, he would go where other people were making it, and where it would not seem so unnatural as it would in the secular repose of Florence, among those who had all put off their armor at the close of the sixteenth century. [Garofalo alleged the intellectual activity everywhere around him in science, literature, philosophy.] Olney could not say that it seemed to him a life referred from Germany, France and England, without root in Italian soil ; but he could answer that all this might very well be without affording a lucrative practice for a specialist in nervous diseases, who could be most prosperous where nervous diseases most abounded.

The question was joked away between them, and in the end there never seemed to have been any very serious question of Olney's staying in Florence. Now, if there had not been really, he wished there really had been. Everything discouraged him, somehow ; and no doubt his depression was partly a physical mood. He had never expected to find people in town at that time in the summer, or to begin practice at once; he had only promised himself to look about and be suitably settled to receive the nervous sufferers when they began to get back in the fall. Yet the sight of all those handsome houses on the Back Bay, where nervous suffering, if it were to avail him, must mainly abide, struck a chill to his spirit; they seemed to repel his intended ministrations with their barricaded doorways and their close-shuttered windows. His failure to find Dr. Wingate, with whom he had advised about his studies, and with whom he had hoped to talk over his hopes, was peculiarly disheartening, though when he reasoned with himself he saw that there was an imperative logic in Wingate's absence; a nervous specialist of his popularity must, of course, have followed nervous suffering somewhere out of town. Still it was a disappointment, and it made the expense of Olney's sojourn seem yet more ruinous. The hotel where he had gone for cheapness was an old house kept on the American plan; but his outgo of three dollars a day dismayed him when he thought of the *arrangiamento* he could have made in Florence for half the money. He determined to look up a boarding-house in the morning; and the thought of this made him almost sick.

 Olney was no longer so young as he had been; we none of us are as young as we once were; but all of us have not reached the great age of thirty, as he had, after seeming sweetly destined to remain forever in the twenties. He belonged to a family that became bald early, and there was already a thin place in the hair on his crown, which he discovered one day when he was looking at the back of his head in the glass. It was shortly after the Union Pacific first passed its dividend, and it made him feel for the time decrepit. Yet he was by no means superannuated in other respects. His color was youthfully fresh; his soft full beard was of a rich golden red; what there was of his hair — and there was by no means little except in that one spot — was of the same mellow color, which it would keep till forty, without a touch of gray. His figure had not lost its youthful slimness, and it looked even fashionable in its clothes of London cut; so that any fellow-countryman who disliked his air of reserve might easily have passed him by on the other side, and avoided him for a confounded Englishman.

He sat on the high-pillared portico of the hotel, smoking for a half-hour after he returned from his evening stroll, and then he went to his room, and began to go to bed. He was very meditative about it, and after he took off his coat, he sat on the edge of the bed, pensively holding one shoe in his hand, until he could think to unlace the other.

III.

THERE came a shattering knock at his door, such as rouses you in the night when the porter mistakes your number for that of the gentleman he was to call at four. Olney shouted, "Come in!" and sat waiting the result, with his shoe still in his hand. The door opened and one of those Irish faces showed itself.

— "Are you a doctor, sor?"—

"Yes."

"Ahl right."

The face was withdrawn, and the door was closing, when Olney called out: "Why? What of it? Does any one want me?"

"I don't know, sor. There's a lady in Twenty-wan that sah your name in the paper; but she said not to disturb ye if ye wahsn't a doctor."

"A lady?" said Olney. He rapidly reasoned that the lady, whoever she was, had found his name printed in the Sunday papers among the arrivals at that hotel, and that she must have some association with it. "Is she ill? Does she know me?"

"I don't know, sor," said the man, with an air of wishing to conceal nothing. "She don't be in bed, annyway."

Olney reflected a moment, hesitating between a certain vexation at being molested with this ridiculous message and a vague curiosity to find out who the lady could be. As a man, he would have wished to know who any unknown woman could be ; as a man of science, he divined that this unknown woman was probably one of those difficult invalids who have to be coaxed into anything decisive, even sending for a doctor ; this tentative question of hers must represent ever so much self-worry and a high degree of self-conquest.

"Tell her, yes, I'm a doctor," he said to the man. He added, for purposes of identification, "Dr. Edward Olney." He thought for an instant he would send his card ; but he decided this would be silly.

"Ah! right, sor. Thank ye, sor," said the man.

He went away, and Olney put on the shoe he had taken off, and got into his coat again. He expected the man back at once, and he wished to be ready, but the messenger did not come for ten or twelve minutes. Then he brought Olney a note, superscribed in a young-lady-like hand, and diffusing when opened a perfume which was instantly but indefinitely memoriferous. Where had he last met the young lady who used that perfume, so full of character, so redolent of personality ? The mystery was solved by the note, and all the pleasure of the writer's presence returned to him at the sight of her name.

"DEAR SIR, — My aunt, Mrs. Meredith, is so very far from well, that she asks me to write for her, and

2

beg you to come and see her. She hopes she is not mistaken in thinking it is Dr. Olney whom she met at Professor Garofalo's in Florence last winter; but if it is not, she trusts you will pardon the intrusion, other. wise unwarrantable at such an hour.

Yours very truly,
Rhoda Aldgate."

"Where is the room?" Olney demanded, putting the note into his breast pocket, and taking up his hat. He smiled to think how much less distinctive the diction was than the perfume; he fancied that Miss Aldgate had written down her aunt's words, which had a formality alien to the nature of the young girl he remembered so agreeably. As he followed along through the apparently aimless corridors, up and down short flights of steps that seemed to ascend at one point only to descend at another, he recalled the particulars of her beauty; her slender height, her rich complexion of olive, with a sort of under-stain of red, and the inky blackness of her eyes and hair. Her face was of almost classic perfection, and the hair, crinkling away to either temple, grew low upon the forehead, as the hair does in the Clytie head. In profile the mouth was firmly accented, with a deep cut outlining the full lower lip, and a fine jut forward of the delicate chin; and the regularity of the mask was farther relieved from insipidity by the sharp wing-like curve in the sides of the sensitive nostrils. Olney recalled it as a mask, and he recalled his sense of her

wearing this family face, with its somewhat tragic
beauty, over a personality that was at once gentle and
gay. The mask, he felt, was inherited, but the character seemed to be of Miss Aldgate's own invention,
and expressed itself in the sunny sparkle of her looks,
that ran over with a willingness to please and to be
pleased, and to consist in effect of a succession of
flashing, childlike smiles, showing between her red
lips teeth of the milkiest whiteness, small, even and
perfect. These looks, the evening he remembered
first meeting her and her aunt, were employed chiefly
upon a serious young clergyman, sojourning in Florence after a journey to the Holy Land. But they
were not employed coquettishly so much as sympa-
thetically, with a readiness for laughter that broke up
the inherited mask with a strange contradictory levity.
Olney was himself immersed in a long and serious
analysis of *Romola* with the aunt, who appeared to
have a conscience of prodigious magnifying force, cul-
tivated to the last degree by a constant training upon
the ethical problems of fiction. She brought its powerful lenses to bear upon the most intimate particles of
Tito's character; his bad qualities seemed to give her
almost as much satisfaction as if they had been her
own. In knocking at Mrs. Meredith's door, he now
remembered how charmingly that pretty little head of
Miss Aldgate's, defined by the black hair with its lustrous crinkle, was set upon her shoulders.

IV.

THE young girl herself opened the door, and faced him first with the tragic family mask. Then she put out her hand to him with the personal gayety he had recalled. Her laugh, so far as it bore upon the situation, recognized rather the good joke of their finding themselves all in an American hotel together than expressed anxiety for her aunt's condition. It was so glad and free, in fact, that Olney was surprised to find Mrs. Meredith looking quite haggard on the sofa, from which she reached him her hand without attempting to rise.

"Isn't it the most fortunate thing in the world," said Miss Aldgate, "that it should *really* be Dr. Olney? We couldn't believe it when we saw it in the paper!" she added; and now Olney perceived that the laugh which he might have thought indifferent, was a laugh of happy relief, of trust that since it was he, all must go well.

"Yes, it is indeed," said Mrs. Meredith; but she had none of the gayety in putting the burden upon Olney, under Providence, which flashed out in her niece's smile; she appeared to doubt whether Providence and he could manage it, and to relinquish it with misgiving. "There were so many chances against it that it scarcely seemed possible." She examined Olney's face, which had at once begun to hide the professional opinion he was forming, and seemed to find comfort in its unsmiling strength. "And I hated dreadfully to trouble you at such an hour."

"I believe there's no etiquette as to the time of a doctor's visits," said Olney, pulling a chair up to the sofa, and looking down at her. "I hope, if things go well after I'm settled here, to be called up sometimes in the middle of the night, though ten o'clock isn't bad for my second day in Boston." Miss Aldgate laughed with instant appreciation of his pleasantry, and Mrs. Meredith wanly smiled. "You must be even more recent than I am, Mrs. Meredith. I'm afraid that if I had found your names in the register when I signed mine, I should have ventured to call unprofessionally. But then it would very likely have been some other Mrs. Meredith."

Miss Aldgate laughed again, and Olney gave her a look of the kindness a man feels for any one who sees his joke. She dropped upon the chair at the head of the sofa, and invited him with dancing eyes to say some more of those things. But Mrs. Meredith took the word.

"We only got in this morning. That is, the steamer arrived too late last night for us to come ashore, and we drove to the hotel before breakfast. You must be rather surprised to find us in such a place."

"Not at all; I'm here myself," said Olney.

"Oh!" Miss Aldgate laughed.

"I don't assume," he added, "that you came here for cheapness, as I did. At the hotels on the European plan, as they call it, they charge you as much for a room as they do for room and board together here."

"Everything is very expensive," sighed Mrs. Meredith. "We paid three dollars for our carriage from the ship; and I believe it's nothing to what it is in New York. But it's a great while since I've been in Boston, and I told them to bring me here because I'd heard it was an old-fashioned, quiet place. I felt the need of rest, but it seems very noisy. It was very smooth all the way over; but I was excited, and I slept badly. The last two or three nights I've scarcely slept at all."

"Hmm!" said the doctor, feeling himself launched upon the case.

Miss Aldgate rose.

"My dear," said her aunt, "I wish you would look up the prescription the ship's doctor gave me. I was thinking of sending out to have it made up, but I shouldn't wish to try it now unless Dr. Olney approves."

Olney profited by Miss Aldgate's absence to feel Mrs. Meredith's pulse and look at her tongue. He asked her a few formal questions. He was a little surprised to find her so much better than she looked.

"You seem a little upset, Mrs. Meredith," he said. "You may be suffering from suppressed seasickness,

but I don't think it's anything worse." He tried
to treat the affair lightly, and he added : "I don't see
why you shouldn't be on good terms with sleep. You
know Tito slept very well, even with a bad conscience."

Mrs. Meredith would not smile with him at the
recurrence to their last conversation. She sighed,
and gave him a look of tragical appeal. "I sometimes think he had an enviable character."

"Or temperament," Olney suggested. "There
doesn't seem to have been much question of character.
But he was certainly well constituted for getting on in
a world where there was no moral law — if he could
have found such a world."

"Then you do believe there *is* such a law in *this*
world?" Mrs. Meredith demanded, with an intensity
that did not flatter Olney he had been light to good
purpose.

He could not help smiling at his failure. "I would
rather not say till you had got a night's rest."

"No, no," she persisted. "Do you believe that any
one can rightfully live a lie? Do you believe that
Tito was ever really at rest when he thought of what
he was concealing?"

"He seems to have been pretty comfortable, except
when Romola got at him with her moral nature."

"Ah, don't laugh!" said Mrs. Meredith. "It isn't
a thing to laugh at."

Miss Aldgate came in, with a scrap of paper flutter-
ing from her slim hand, and showing her pretty teeth

in a smile so free of all ethical question that Olney
swiftly conjectured an anxiety of Mrs. Meredith concerning a nature so apparently free of all personal
responsibility as the young girl looked at that moment. He was aware of innocently rejoicing in this
sense of her, which came from the goodness and sweetness which she looked as much as the irresponsibility.
It might be that Mrs. Meredith had lost sleep in
revolving the problems of Miss Aldgate's character,
and the chances of her being equal to the duties that
had left so little of Mrs. Meredith. If such an aunt
and such a niece were formed to wear upon each
other, as the ladies say, it was clear that the niece had
worn the most. With this thought evanescently in
mind, Olney took the prescription from her.

He read it over, but he did not perceive that the
sense of it had failed to reach his mind till Mrs. Meredith said, " If it is one of those old-fashioned narcotics
— he called it a sleeping draught — I would rather
not take it."

Though Olney had not been thinking of the prescription, he now pretended that he had. " It would
be rather a heroic dose for a first-cabin passenger," he
said, " though it might do for the steerage." He took
out his pocket-book and wrote a prescription himself.
" There! I think that ought to get you a night's rest,
Mrs. Meredith."

" I suppose we can get it made up ? " she said, irres-
olutely, lifting herself a little on one elbow.

" I'll take it out and have it done myself," said

Olney. "There's an apothecary's just under the hotel."

He rose, but she said: "I can't let you be at that trouble. We can send. Will you —"

"I will ring, Aunt Caroline," said Miss Aldgate; and she ran forward to press the electric button by the door.

The bell was answered by the same man who came to call the doctor to Mrs. Meredith. Miss Aldgate took the prescription, and rapidly explained to him what she wanted. When she had finished, he looked up from the prescription at Olney with a puzzled face.

Olney smiled and Miss Aldgate laughed. The man had not understood at all.

"You know the apothecary's shop under the hotel?" Olney began.

"Yes, I know that forst-rate, sor."

"Well, take that paper down and give it to the apothecary, and wait till he makes up the medicine, and then bring it back to us."

"This paper, sor?"

"No; the medicine."

"And lave the paper wid um?"

"Yes. The apothecary will give you the medicine and keep the prescription. Do you understand?"

"Yes, sor."

"Well?"

"Is the 'pot'ecary after havin' the prescription now, sor?"

Olney took the paper out of his hand and shook it at him. "This paper — this — is the prescription. Do you understand?"

"Yes, sor."

"Take it to the apothecary —"

"The man under the hotel, sor?"

"Yes, the one under the hotel. This prescription — this paper — give it to him; and he will make up a medicine, and give it to you in a bottle; and then you bring it here."

"The bottle, sor?"

"Yes, the bottle with the medicine in it."

"Ahl right, sor! I understand, sor!"

The man hurried away down the corridor, and Miss Aldgate shut the door and broke into a laugh at sight of Olney's face, red and heated with the effort he had been making.

Olney laughed too. "If the matter had been much simpler, I never should have got it into his head at all!"

"They seem to have *no* imagination!" said the girl.

"Or too much," suggested Olney. "There is something very puzzling to us Teutons in the Celtic temperament. We don't know where to have an Irishman. We can predicate of a brother Teuton that this will please him, and that will vex him, but we can't of an Irishman. You treat him with the greatest rudeness and he doesn't mind it; then you propose to be particularly kind and nice, and he takes fire with the most bewildering offence."

"I *know* it," said Miss Aldgate. "That was the way with all our cooks in New York. Don't you remember, aunty?"

Mrs. Meredith made no answer, and

"We can't call them stupid," Olney went on. "I think that as a general thing the Irish are quicker-witted than we are. They're sympathetic and poetic far beyond us. [But they can't understand the simplest thing from us.] Perhaps they set the high constructive faculties of the imagination at work, when they ought to use a little attention and mere common-sense. At any rate they seem more foreign to our intelligence, our way of thinking, than the Jews — or the negroes even."

"Oh, I'm glad to hear you say that about the negroes," said Miss Aldgate. "We were having a dispute this afternoon," she explained, "about the white waiters here and the colored waiters at the Hotel Vendome. I was calling on some friends we have there," and Miss Aldgate flushed a little as she said this: "or rather, they came here to see us, and then I drove back with them a moment; and it made me quite homesick to come away and leave those black waiters. Don't you think they're charming? With those soft voices and gentle manners? My aunt has no patience with me; she can't bear to have me look at them; but I never see one of them without loving them. I suppose it's because they're about the first thing I can remember. I was born in the South, you know. Perhaps I got to having a sort of fellow-feeling with them from my old black nurse. You know the Italians say you do."

She turned vividly toward Olney, as if to refer the scientific point to him, but he put it by with a laugh.

"I'm afraid I feel about them as Miss Aldgate does, Mrs. Meredith; and I hadn't an old black nurse, either. I've been finding them delightful, wherever I've seen them, since I got back." Miss Aldgate clapped her hands. "To be sure, I haven't been here long enough to get tired of them."

"Oh, I should *never* tire of them!" said the girl.

"But so far, certainly, they seem to me the most agreeable, the most interesting feature of the social spectacle."

"There, Aunt Caroline!"

"I must confess," Olney went on, "that it's given me a distinct pleasure whenever I've met one of them. They seem to be the only people left who have any heart for life here; they all look hopeful and happy, even in the rejection from their fellow-men, which strikes me as one of the most preposterous, the most monstrous things in the world, now I've got back to it here."

Mrs. Meredith lay with her hand shading her eyes and half her face. She asked, without taking her hand away, "Would you like to meet them on terms of social equality — intermarry with them?"

"Oh, now, Aunt Caroline!" Miss Aldgate broke in. "Who's talking of anything like that?"

"I certainly am not," said Olney, "as far as the

intermarrying is concerned. [But short of that I don't see why one shouldn't associate with them. There are terms a good deal short of the affection we lavish on dogs and horses that I fancy they might be very glad of. We might recognize them as fellow-beings in public, if we don't in private; but we ignore, if we don't repulse them at every point — from our business as well as our bosoms.] Yes, it strikes one as very odd on getting home — very funny, very painful. You would think we might meet on common ground before our common God — but we don't. They have their own churches, and I suppose it would be as surprising to find one of them at a white communion-table as it would to find one at a white dinner-party."

KEY POINT

Olney said this without the least feeling about the matter, except a sense of its grotesqueness. He was himself an agnostic, but he could be as censorious of the Christians who denied Christ in the sacrament, as if he had himself been a better sort. He added:

agnostic

"Possibly the negroes would be welcome in a Catholic church; the Catholics seem to have kept the ideal of Christian equality in their churches. If ever they turn their attention to the negroes — "

"Oh, I can't imagine a colored Catholic," said Miss Aldgate. "There seems something unnatural in the very idea."

"All the same, there are a good many of them."

"In Boston?"

"No, not in Boston, I fancy."

Mrs. Meredith had taken no farther part in the conversation; she lay rigidly quiet on her sofa, with her hand shading her eyes.

There was a knock at the door, and Miss Aldgate sprang to open it, with the effect of being glad to work off her exuberant activity in that or any other way: with Mrs. Meredith so passive, and Olney so acquiescent, the discussion of the race problem was not half enough for her.

The man was there, with the bottle from the apothecary's, and he and Miss Aldgate had a beaming little interview. He exulted in getting back with the medicine all right, and she gratefully accepted his high sense of his offices, and repaid him his outlay, running about the room, and opening several trunks and bags to find her purse, and then added something for his trouble.

"Dear me!" she said, when she got rid of him, "I wish they wouldn't make it *quite* so clear that they expected to be 'remembered.' They've kept my memory on the *qui vive* every moment I've been in the hotel."

Olney smiled in sympathy as he took the bottle from her. "I've found it impossible to forget the least thing they've done for me, and I never boasted of my memory."

She stood watching his examination of the label of the bottle, and his test of its contents from a touch of the inner tip of the cork on his tongue. "A spoon? I've got one here in aunty's medicine chest. It would have cost its weight in silver to get one from the dining-room. And there happens to be ice-water, if you have to give it in water. *Don't* say water without ice!"

"Ice-water will do," said Olney. He began to drop the medicine from the bottle into the spoon, which he then poured into the glass of water she brought him. "I believe," he said, stirring it, "that if the negroes ever have their turn — and if the meek are to inherit the earth they must come to it — we shall have a civilization of such sweetness and good-will as the world has never known yet. Perhaps we shall have to wait their turn for any real Christian civilization."

the meek
Shall inherit
the earth

"You remember the black Madonna at Florence, that used to be so popular? What Madonna was it? I suppose they will revere *her*, when they get to be all Catholics. Were you in any of their churches to-day? You were saying —" Miss Aldgate put out her hand for the glass.

"No; I never was in a colored church in my life," said Olney. ["I'm critical, not constructive, in my humanity. It's easier."]

He went himself with the glass to Mrs. Meredith. She seemed not to have been paying any attention to his talk with her niece. She lifted herself up at his approach, and took the glass from him.

"Shall I drink it all?"

"Yes — you can take all of it."

She quaffed it at one nervous gulp, and flung her head heavily down again. "I don't believe it will make me sleep," she said.

Olney smiled. "Well, fortunately, this kind doesn't require the co-operation of the patient. It will make you sleep, I think. You may try keeping awake, if you like."

She opened her eyes with a flash. "Is it chloral?"

"No, it isn't chloral."

"Tell me the truth!" She laid a convulsive clutch upon his wrist, as he sat fronting her and curiously watching her. "I will not let you justify yourself by that code of yours which lets the doctor cheat his patient! If you have been giving me some form of chloral —"

"I haven't been giving you any form of chloral," said Olney, beginning to smile.

"Then you are trying to hypnotize me!"

Olney burst into a laugh. "You certainly need sleep, Mrs. Meredith! I'll look in during the forenoon, about the time you ought to wake, and dehypnotize you." He moved toward the door; but before he reached it he stopped and said, seriously: "I don't know of any code that would allow me to cheat you, against your will. I don't believe any doctor is justified in doing that. Unless he has some sign, some petition for deception, from the patient, you can depend upon it that he finds the truth the best thing."

"It's the only thing — at all times — in life and death!" cried Mrs. Meredith, perfervidly. "If I were dying, I should wish to know it!"

"And I *shouldn't* wish to know it!" said Miss Aldgate. "I think there are cases when the truth would be cruel — positively wicked! Don't you, Dr. Olney?"

"Well," said Olney, preparing to escape through the door which he had set open, "I couldn't honestly say that I think either of us is in immediate danger. Good-night!"

3

V.

Olney did not go to see Mrs. Meredith until noon, the next day. He thought that if she were worse, or no better, she would send for him, and that if she did not send, he might very well delay seeing her. He found her alone. Miss Aldgate, she said, had gone to drive with their friends at the Vendome, and was to lunch with them. Olney bore her absence as politely as he could, and hoped Mrs. Meredith had slept.

"Yes, I slept," she said, with a kind of suppressed sigh, "but I'm not sure that I'm very much the better for it."

"I'm sure you are," said Olney, with resolute cheerfulness; and he began to go through with the usual touching of the pulse, and looking at the tongue, and the questions that accompany this business.

Mrs. Meredith broke abruptly away from it all. "It's useless for us to go on! I've no doubt you can drug me to sleep whenever you will. But if I'm to wake up, when I wake, to the trouble that's on my mind, the sleep will do me no good."

She looked wistfully at him, as if she longed to have him ask her what the matter was; but Olney did not feel authorized to do this. He had known, almost from the first moment he met Mrs. Meredith, the night before, that she had something on her mind, or believed so, and that if she could tell him of her trouble, she would probably need no medicine; but he had to proceed, as the physician often must, upon the theory that only her body was out of order, and try to quiet her spirit through her nerves, when the true way was from the other direction. It went through his mind that it might be well for the nervous specialist hereafter to combine the functions of the priest and the leech, especially in the case of nervous ladies, and confess his patients before he began to prescribe for them.

But he could not help feeling glad that things had not come to this millennial pass; for he did not at all wish to know what Mrs. Meredith had on her mind. So much impression of her character had been left from their different meetings in Florence that he had already theorized her as one of those women, commoner amongst us than any other people, perhaps, to whom life, in spite of all experience, remains a sealed book, and who are always trying to unlock its mysteries with the keys furnished them by fiction. (They judge the world by the novels they have read, and their acquaintance in the flesh by characters in stories, instead of judging these by the real people they have met, and more or less lived with.] Such women get a tone of mind that is very tiresome to every one but other women like them, and that is peculiarly repulsive to such men as Olney, or if not repulsive, then very ridiculous. In Mrs. Meredith's case he did not so much accuse her of wishing to pose as a character

with a problem to work out; there was nothing histri-
onic about the poor woman; but he fancied her hopelessly muddled as to her plain, every-day obligations,
by a morbid sympathy with the duty-ridden creatures
of the novelist's brain. He remembered from that
first talk of the winter before — it had been a long
talk, an exhaustive talk, covering many cases of conscience in fiction besides that of Tito Malema — that
she had shown herself incapable of sinking the sense
of obligation in the sense of responsibility, and that
she apparently conceived of what she called living up
to the truth as something that might be done singly;
that right affected her as a body of positive color,
sharply distinguished from wrong, and not shading
into and out of it by gradations of tint, as we find it
doing in reality. Such a woman, he had vaguely reflected, when he came to sum up his impressions, would
be capable of an atrocious cruelty in speaking or acting the truth, and would consider herself an exemplary
person for having done her duty at any cost of suffering to herself and others. But she would exaggerate
as well as idealize, and he tried to find comfort now in
thinking that what she had on her mind was very
likely a thing of bulk out of all proportion to its
weight. Very likely it was something with reference
to her niece; some waywardness of affection or ambition in the girl. She might be wanting to study
medicine, or law, or divinity; perhaps she wanted to
go on the stage. More probably, it was a question of
whom she should marry, and Mrs. Meredith was

wrestling with the problem of how far in this age of intense individualization a girl's inclinations might be forced for her good, and how far let go for her evil. Such a problem would be quite enough to destroy Mrs. Meredith's peace, if that was what she had on her mind; and Olney could not help relating his conjecture to these people at the Vendome, whom Miss Aldgate had gone to drive with and lunch with to-day, after having been to drive with them yesterday. Those people in turn he related to the young clergyman she had spent the evening in talking with in Florence, when he was himself only partially engaged in exploring her aunt's conscience. He wondered whether Mrs. Meredith favored or opposed the young clergyman, and what was just the form of the trouble that was on her mind, but still without the intention to inquire it out.

"Well, perhaps," he suggested, half jocosely, "the trouble will disappear when you've had sleep enough."

"You know very well," she answered, "that it won't — that what you say is simply impossible. I remember some things you said that night when we talked so long together, and I know that you are inclined to confound the moral and the physical, as all doctors are."

Olney would have liked to say, "I wish, my dear lady, you wouldn't confound the sane and insane in the way you do." But he silently submitted, and let her go on.

"That made me dislike you; but I can't say it made

me distrust you. I think that if you had been an un-
truthful person you would have concealed your point
of view from me."

Olney could not say he might not have thought it
worth while to do that. On the contrary, he had a
sort of compassion for the lofty superiority of a woman
who so obviously felt her dependence upon him, and
was arming herself in all her pride for her abasement
before him. He knew that she was longing to tell
him what was on her mind, and would probably not
end till she had done it. He did not feel that he had
the right to prevent her doing that, and he smiled pas-
sively in saying, " I couldn't advise you to trust me too
far."

" I must trust *some* one too far," she said, "and I
have literally no one but you." The tears came into
her eyes, and Olney, who knew very well how easily
the tears come into women's eyes, was broken up by
the sight.

" My dear Mrs. Meredith, I should be very glad to
be trusted even too far, if I could really be of use to
you."

"Oh, I don't know that you can," she said. After
a pause she added, abruptly, " Do you believe in
heredity ? "

Olney felt inclined to laugh. " Well, that's rather
a spacious question, Mrs. Meredith. What do you
mean by heredity ? "

" You know ! The persistence of ancestral traits ;
the transmission of character and tendency ; the

reappearance of types after several generations; the — "

She stopped, and Olney knew that he had got at the body of her anxiety, though she had not yet revealed its very features. He determined to deal with the matter as reassuringly as he could in the dark. He smiled in answering, "Heredity is a good deal like the germ theory. There's a large amount of truth in it, no doubt; but it's truth in a state of solution, and nobody knows just how much of it there is. Perhaps we shall never know. As for those cases of atavism — for I suppose that's what you mean — "

"Yes, yes! Atavism? That is the word."

"They're not so very common, and they're not so very well ascertained. You find them mentioned in the books, but vaguely, and on a kind of hearsay, without the names of persons and places; it's a notion that some writers rather like to toy with; but when you come to boil it down, as the newspapers say, there isn't a great deal of absolute fact there. Take the reversion to the inferior race type in the child of parents of mixed blood — say a white with a mulatto or quadroon — "

"Yes!" said Mrs. Meredith, with eagerness.

"Why, it's very effective as a bit of drama. But it must be very rare — very rare indeed. You hear of instances in which the parent of mixed race could not be known from a white person, and yet the child reverts to the negro type in color and feature and character. I should doubt it very much."

Mrs. Meredith cried out as if he had questioned holy writ. "You should doubt it! Why should you doubt it, Dr. Olney?" Yet he perceived that for some reason she wished him to reaffirm his doubt.

"Because the chances are so enormously against it. The natural tendency is all the other way, to the permanent effacement of the inferior type. The child of a white and an octoroon is a sixteenth blood; and the child of that child and a white is a thirty-second blood. The chances of atavism, or reversion to the black great-great-great-grandfather are so remote that they may be said hardly to exist at all. They are outside of the probabilities, and only on the verge of the possibilities. But it's so thrilling to consider such a possibility that people like to consider it. Fancy is as much committed to it as prejudice is; but it hasn't so much excuse, for prejudice is mostly ignorant, and fancy mostly educated, or half-educated." Olney folded one leg comfortably across the other, and went on, with a musing smile. "I've been thinking about all this a good deal within the past two days — or since I got back to Boston. I've been more and more struck with the fact that sooner or later our race must absorb the colored race; and I believe that it will obliterate not only its color, but its qualities. The tame man, the civilized man, is stronger than the wild man; and I believe that in those cases within any one race where there are very strong ancestral proclivities on one side especially toward evil, they will die out before the good tendencies on the other side, for much the same reason, that is, because vice is savage and virtue is civilized."

Mrs. Meredith listened intently, but at last, "I wish I could believe what you say," she sighed, heavily. "But I don't know that that would relieve me of the duty before me," she added, after a moment's thought. "Dr. Olney, there is something that I need very much to speak about — something that must be done — that my health depends upon — I shall never get well unless — "

"If there is anything you wish to say concerning your health, Mrs. Meredith," he answered, seriously, "it's of course my duty to hear it."

He sat prepared to listen, but she apparently did not know how to begin, and after several gasps she was silent. Then, "No, I can't tell you!" she broke out.

He rose. "Are you to be some time in Boston?" he asked, to relieve the embarrassment of the situation.

"I don't know. Yes, I suppose a week or two."

"If I can be of use to you in any way, I shall be glad to have you send for me."

He turned to the door, but as he put his hand on the knob she called out: "No! Don't go! Sit down! I must speak! You remember," she hurried on, before he could resume his chair, "a young gentleman who talked with my niece that night at Professor Garofalo's — a Mr. Bloomingdale?"

"The young minister?"

"Yes."

"I remember him very well, though I don't think I spoke with him."

Olney stared at Mrs Meredith, wondering what this Rev. Mr. Bloomingdale had to do with the matter, whatever the matter might be.

"It is his mother and sisters that my niece is lunching with," she said, with an air of explaining. "He is expected on the next steamer, and then — then I must speak! It can't go on, so. There must be a clear and perfect understanding. Dr. Olney," she continued, with a glance at his face, which he felt growing more and more bewildered under the influence of her words, "Mr. Bloomingdale is very much attached to my niece. He — he has offered himself; he offered himself in Liverpool; and I insisted that Rhoda should not give him a decisive answer then — that she should take time to think it over. I wished to gain time myself."

"Yes," said Olney, because she seemed to expect him to say something.

"I wished to gain time and I wished to gain strength, but I have lost both; and the affair has grown more difficult and complicated. Mr. Bloomingdale's family are very fond of Rhoda; they are aware of his attachment — they were in Florence at the time you were, and they came home without him a few months ago, because he wished to stay on in the hope of winning her — and they are showing her every attention; and she does not see how her being with them complicates everything. Of course they flatter her, and she's very headstrong, like all young girls, and I'm afraid she's committing herself — "

" Do they live at the Vendome? " Olney asked, with a certain distaste for them, and he was conscious of resenting their attentions to Miss Aldgate as pushing and vulgar under the circumstances, though he had no right to do so.

" No. They are just waiting there for him. They are New York State people — the western part. They are very rich ; the mother is a widow, and they are going to live in Ohio, where Mr. Bloomingdale has a call. They are kind, good people — very kind ; and I feel that Rhoda is abusing their kindness by being so much with them before she has positively accepted him ; and I can't let her do that until everything is known. She refused him when he offered himself first in Florence — I've always thought she had some other fancy — but at Liverpool, where he renewed his offer just before we sailed, she was inclined to accept him ; I suppose her fancy had passed. As I say, I insisted that she should take at least a week to consider it, and that he should change his passage from our steamer to the next. I had no idea of finding his family in Boston, but perhaps in the confusion he forgot to tell us. They found our names in the passenger list, and they came to see us directly after lunch, yesterday. If the match is broken off now, after — "

Mrs. Meredith stopped in a sort of despair, which Olney shared with her as far as concerned the blind alley in which he found himself. He had not the least notion of the way out, and he could only wait her motion.

"I don't see," she resumed, "how my niece can help accepting him if she goes on at this rate with his family, and I don't know how to stop her without telling her the worst at once. I'm afraid she has got her heart set on him." Mrs. Meredith paused again, and then went on. "I have shrunk from speaking because I know that the poor young man's happiness, as well as Rhoda's, is involved, and the peace and self-respect of his family. There have been times when I have almost felt that if there were no danger of the facts ever coming to light, I could make up my mind to die, as I have lived, in a lie. But now I know I cannot; it is my duty to speak out; and the marriage must not take place unless everything is known. It will kill her. But it must be done ! Those ancestral traits, those tendencies, may die out, but I can't let any one take the risk of their recurrence unknowingly. He must know who and what she is as fully as I do: her origin, her —"

Olney believed that he began to understand. There was some stain upon that poor child's birth. She was probably not related to Mrs. Meredith at all ; she was a foundling ; or she was the daughter of some man or woman whose vices or crimes might find her out with their shame if not their propensity some day. Whatever sinister tendency she was heiress to, or whatever ancestral infamy, it could only be matter of conjecture,

not inquiry, with Olney; but he imagined the worst
from hints that Mrs. Meredith had thrown out, and
attributed her to a family of criminals, such as has here
and there found its way into the figures of the statis-
ticians. He was not shocked; he was interested by
the fact; and he did not find Miss Aldgate at all less
charming and beautiful in the conclusion he jumped to
than he had found her before. He said to himself
that if the case were his, as it was that young minister's, there could be no question in it, except the question of her willingness to marry him. He said this
from the safe vantage of the disinterested witness,
and with the easy decision of one who need not act
upon his decision.

VI.

In his instantaneous mental processes, Olney kept his attention fixed upon Mrs. Meredith, and he was aware of her gasping out:

"My niece is of negro descent."

Olney recoiled from the words, in a turmoil of emotion for which there is no term but disgust. His disgust was profound and pervasive, and it did not fail, first of all, to involve the poor child herself. He found himself personally disliking the notion of her having negro blood in her veins; before he felt pity he felt repulsion; his own race instinct expressed itself in a merciless rejection of her beauty, her innocence, her helplessness because of her race. The impulse had to have its course; and then he mastered it, with an abiding compassion, and a sort of tender indignation. He felt that it was atrocious for this old woman to have allowed her hypochondriacal anxiety to dabble with the mysteries of the young girl's future in that way, and he resented having been trapped into considering her detestable question. His feeling was unscientific; but he could not at once detach himself from the purely social relation which he had hitherto held toward Miss Aldgate. The professional view which he was invited to take seemed to have lost all dignity,

to be impertinent, cruel, squalid, and to involve the
abdication of certain sentiments, conventions, which he
was unwilling to part with, at least in her case.
Sensibilities which ought not to have survived his
scientific training and ambition were wounded to re-
bellion in him; he perceived as never before that
there was an inherent outrage in the submission of
such questions to one of the opposite sex; there should
be women to deal with them.

"How — negro descent?" he asked, stupidly, from
the whirl of these thoughts.

"I will try to tell you," said Mrs. Meredith. "And
some things you said about that — race — those
wretched beings, last night — You were sincere in
what you said?" she demanded of the kind of change
that came into his face.

"Sincere? Yes," said Olney, thinking how far
from any concrete significance he had supposed his
words to have for his listeners when he spoke them.
He added, "I do abhor the cruel stupidity that makes
any race treat another as outcast. But I never
dreamed — "

Mrs. Meredith broke in upon him, saying:

"It is almost the only consolation I have in think-
ing she is rightfully and lawfully |my niece, to know
that in the course I must take now, I shall not be
seeming to make her an outcast. I honored my
brother for honoring her mother, and giving her his
name when there was no need of his doing it   He did
not consult me, and I did not know it till afterward;

but I should have been the first to urge it, when it came to a question of marriage or — anything else. For one of our family there could *be* no such question ; there was none for him.

"He went South shortly after the war, as so many Northern men did, intending to make his home there ; his health was delicate, and his only hope of strength and usefulness, if not of life, was in a milder climate. He outlived the distrust that the Southerners had for all Northern men in those days, and was establishing himself in a very good practice at New Orleans — I forgot to say he was a physician — when he met Rhoda's mother. I needn't go over the details ; she was an <u>octoroon</u>, the daughter and the granddaughter of women who had never hoped for marriage with the white men who fell in love with them ; but she had been educated by her father — he was a Creole, and she was educated in a Northern convent — and I have no doubt she was an accomplished and beautiful girl. I never saw her. My brother met her in her father's house, almost beside her father's death-bed ; but even if he had met her in her mother's house, on her mother's level, it would not have been possible for him to do otherwise than as he did. He thought at first of keeping the marriage secret, and of going on as before, until he could afford to own it and take all the consequences ; but he decided against this, and I was always glad that he did. They were married, after her father's death ; and then my brother's ruin began. He lost his practice in the families where he had got a footing, among the well-to-do and respectable people whom he had made his friends; and though he would have been willing to go on among a poorer class who could pay less, it was useless. He had to go away; and for five or six years he drifted about from one place to another, trying to gain a hold here and there, and failing everywhere. Sooner or later his story followed him.

"I don't blame the Southern people; I'm not sure it would have been better in the North. If it had been known who his wife was, she would not have been received socially here any more than she was there; and I doubt if it would not have affected my brother's professional standing in much the same way. People don't like to think there is anything strange about their doctor; they must make a confidant, they must make a familiar of him; and if there is anything peculiar, unusual— My husband was a very good man, one of the best men who ever lived, and he approved of my brother's marriage in the abstract as much as I did; but even he never liked to think *whom* he had married. He was always afraid it would come out among our friends, somehow, and it would be known that his sister-in-law was —

"At last the poor young creature died, and my brother came North with his little girl. We hoped that then he might begin again, and make a new start in life. But it was too late. He was a mere wreck physically, and he died too within the year. And then it became a question what we should do with the
4

child. As long as she was so merely a child, it was comparatively simple. We had no children of our own, and when my brother died in another part of the State — we were living in New York then, and he had gone up into the Adirondack region in the hope of getting better — it was natural that we should take the little one home. In a place like New York, nothing is known unless you make it known, and Rhoda was brought up in our house, without any conjecture or curiosity from people outside ; she was my brother's orphan, and nobody knew or cared who my brother was ; she had teachers and she had schools like any other child, and she had the companionships and the social advantages which our own station and money could command.

"At first my husband and I thought of letting her think herself our child; but that would have involved a deceit which we were unwilling to practise ; besides, it was not necessary, and it would have been great pain for her afterwards. We decided to tell her the truth when the time came, and never anything but the truth, at any time. We never deceived her, but we let her deceive herself. When she came to the age when children begin to ask about themselves, we told her that her father had married in the South, and that her mother, whom she did not remember, was of French descent ; but we did not know of her family. This was all true ; but still it was not the truth ; we knew that well enough, but we promised ourselves that when the time came we would tell her the truth.

"She made up little romances about her mother, which she came to believe in as facts, with our sufferance. I should now call it our connivance."

Mrs. Meredith appealed to Olney with a glance, and he said, in the first sympathy he had felt for her, "It was a difficult position."

"She easily satisfied herself — it's astonishing how little curiosity children have about all the mystery of their coming here — and as she had instinctively inferred something strange or unusual about her mother's family, she decided that she had married against her grandfather's wishes. We left her that illusion, too; it seemed so easy to leave things then! It was when she ceased to be a child, and we realized more and more how her life might any time involve some other life, that the question became a constant pressure upon us. Neither my husband or myself ever justified the concealment we lived in concerning her. We often talked of it, and how it must come to an end. But we were very much attached to her, and we put off thinking definitely about the duty before us as long as we could. Sometimes it seemed to us that we ought to tell the child just who and what she was, but we never had the courage; she does not know to this day. What do you think our duty to her really was?"

"Your duty?" Olney echoed, vaguely. A little while ago he would have answered instantly that they had no duty but to keep her in ignorance as long as she lived; but now he could not honestly do this.

The only thing that he could honestly do was to say, "I don't know," and this was what he said.

Mrs. Meredith resumed: "My husband had gone out of business, and there was nothing to keep us at home. But we had nothing definitely in view when we went abroad, or at least nothing explicitly in view. We said that we were going abroad for Rhoda's education; but I think that in my husband's heart, as well as in mine, there was the hope that something might happen to solve the difficulty; we had no plan for solving it. I thought, at any rate, if he did not, that in Europe there would be less unhappiness in store for her than here. I knew that in Europe, especially on the Continent, there was little or none of that race prejudice which we have, and I thought — I imagined — I should find it easier to tell Rhoda the truth, if I could tell her at the same time that it made no difference to the man she was to marry."

Olney understood; and he was rather restive under Mrs. Meredith's apparent helplessness to leave anything to his imagination.

"I hoped it might be some Italian — from the first I liked the Italians the best. We lived a great deal in Italy, at Rome and Naples, at Florence, at Venice, even at Milan; and everywhere we tried to avoid Americans. We went into Italian society almost entirely.

"But it seemed a perfect fatality. Rhoda was always homesick for America, and always eager to meet Americans. She refused all the offers that were

made for her — and they began to come, even before
she was fairly in society — and declared that she would
never marry any one but an American. She was always proclaiming her patriotism, and asserting the
superiority of America over every other country in a
way that would have made anybody but a very pretty
girl offensive. The perplexities simply grew upon us,
and in the midst of them my husband died, and then I
had no one to advise with or confide in. When his
affairs were settled up, it turned out that we were
much poorer than we had believed. For a while I
thought that I should return home, and Rhoda was
always eager to come back, but we staid on at Florence, living very quietly, and we had scarcely been
out at all for a year, when you first met us at Professor Garofalo's. It was there that she met Mr. Bloomingdale, and he was so attentive to her. I could
see at once that he was greatly taken with her, and he
followed up the acquaintance in a way that could not
leave me any doubt. It was certainly not her money
that attracted him.

"I liked him from the beginning; and his being a
minister gave me a kind of hope, I can hardly tell
why. But I thought that if it ever came to my having to tell him about Rhoda, he would be more reasonable. He was so very amiable, very gentle, very
kind. Did you ever meet him afterward, anywhere?"

"No," said Olney, briefly.

"I am sorry; I hoped you had; I thought you
might have come to know him well enough to sug-

gest — I don't like his family, what I've seen of
them, so well. If they know at all what is pending
between him and Rhoda, it doesn't seem very nice of
them to be pursuing her so."

"Mrs. Meredith sat so dreary in her silence that
Olney pitied her, and found a husky voice to say,"
"Perhaps they don't know."

"Perhaps not," she assented, sadly. "But my only
hope now is in his being able to take it, when I tell
him, as I have hardly the hope that any other American would. I must tell him, if she accepts him, or
decides to accept him, and the question is whether I
shall tell him before I tell her. If I tell him first,
fully and frankly, perhaps — perhaps — he may choose
to keep it from her and she need never know. What
— what do you think?" she entreated.

"Really," said Olney, "that's a matter I have no
sort of opinion about. I'm very sorry, but you must
excuse me."

"But you feel that I must tell him?"

"That's another question for you, Mrs. Meredith.
I can't answer it."

She threw herself back on the sofa. "I wish I
were dead! I see no way out of it; and whatever
happens, it will kill the child."

Olney sat silent for some time in a muse almost as
dreary as her own. After having despised her as a
morbid sentimentalist with a hypochondriacal conscience, he had come to respect her, as we respect any
fellow-creature on whom a heavy duty is laid, and

who is struggling faithfully to stand up under the burden. He said suddenly, "You mustn't tell him first, Mrs. Meredith!"

"Why?"

"Because — because — the secret is *hers*, to keep it or to tell it. No one else has the right to know it without her leave."

"And if — if she should choose to keep it from him —not tell him at all?"

"I couldn't blame her. It's no fault, no wrong of hers. And who is to be harmed by its concealment?"

"But the chances — the future — the — the —"

Olney could not bear the recurrence to this phase of the subject. He made a gesture of impatience.

Mrs. Meredith added, with hysterical haste: "It might come out in a hundred ways. I can hear it in her voice at times — it's a *black* voice! I can see it in her looks! I can feel it in her character — so easy, so irresponsible, so fond of what is soft and pleasant! She could not deny herself the amusement of going with those people to-day, though I said all I could against it. She cannot forecast consequences; she's a creature of the present hour; she's like them *all!* I think that in some occult, dreadful way she feels her affinity with them, and that's the reason why she's so attracted by them, so fond of them. It's her race *calling* her! I don't believe she would ever tell him!"

"I think you ought to leave it to her," said Olney.

"And let her live a lie! Oh, I know too well what that is!"

"It's bad. But there may be worse things. It seems as if there might be circumstances in which it was one's *right* to live a lie, as you say; for the sake — "

"Never!" said Mrs. Meredith vehemently. "It is better to die — to kill — than to lie. I know how people say such things and act them, till life is all one web of falsehood, from the rising to the going down of the sun. But I will never consent to be a party to any such deceit. I will tell Rhoda, and then she shall tell me what she is going to do, and if *she* is not going to tell him, *I* will do it. Yes! I will not be responsible for the future, and I should *be* responsible if he did not know. In such a case I could not spare her. She is my own flesh and blood; she is as dear to me as my own child could be; but if she *were* my own child it would be all the same. I would rather see her perish before my eyes than married to any man who did not know the secret of her — O-o-o-o-o!" Mrs. Meredith gave a loud, shuddering cry, as the door was flung suddenly open, and Miss Aldgate flashed radiantly into the room.

She kept the door-knob in her hand, while she demanded, half frightened, half amused, "What in the world is the matter? Did I startle you? Of course! But I just ran in a moment as we were driving by — we're going over to do our duty by Bunker Hill Monument — to see how you were getting on. I'm so glad *you* are here, Dr. Olney." She released the door-knob, and gave him her hand. "Now I can leave

Aunt Caroline without a qualm of conscience till after lunch; and I *did* have a qualm or two, poor aunty!"

She stooped on one knee beside the sofa, and kissed her aunt, who seemed to Olney no better than a murderess in the embrace of her intended victim. In this light and joyous presence, all that he had heard of the girl's anomalous origin became not only incredible, but atrocious. She was purely and merely a young lady, like any other; and he felt himself getting red with shame for having heard what he had been told against his will.

He could not speak, and he marvelled that Mrs, Meredith could command the words to say, in quite an every-day voice: "You silly child! You needn't have stopped. I was getting on perfectly well."

"Of course you were! And I suppose I have interrupted you in the full flow of symptoms! I can imagine what a perfectly delightful time you were having with Dr. Olney! I think I'll change these gloves." She ran into the room that opened from Mrs. Meredith's parlor, and left him unable to lift his eyes from the floor in her brief absence. She came back pulling on one long mousquetaire glove, while the other dangled from her fingers, and began to laugh. "There's one of those colored waiters down there that even *you* couldn't have anything to say against my falling in love with, Aunt Caroline. He's about four feet high, and his feet are about eighteen inches long, so that he looks just like a capital L. He doesn't lift them when he walks, but he slips along on them over the floor like a funny little mouse; I've decided to call him Creepy-Mousy; it just exactly describes him, he's so small and cunning. And he's so sweet! I should like to *own* him, and keep him as long as he lived. Isn't it a shame that we can't *buy* them, Dr. Olney, as we used to do? There! _ I'll put on the other one in the carriage."

She swooped upon her aunt for another kiss, and then flashed out of the room as she had flashed into it, and left Mrs. Meredith and Olney staring at each other.

"Well!" she said. "You see! It is the race instinct! It must assert itself sooner or later."

Olney became suddenly sardonic in the sort of desperation he fell into. "I should say it was the other race instinct that was asserting itself sooner;" and when he had said this he felt somehow a hope, which he tried to impart to Mrs. Meredith.

At the end of all their talk she said: "But that doesn't relieve me of the duty I owe to her and to him. I must tell her, at least, cost what it may. I cannot live this lie any longer. If she chooses to do so, perhaps —"

VII.

Miss Aldgate came in late in the afternoon. She came in softly, and then, finding her aunt awake, she let herself fall into an easy-chair with the air of utter exhaustion that girls like to put on, after getting home from a social pleasure, and sighed out a long "O-o-o-h, dear!"

Her aunt let her sit silent and stare awhile at the carpet just beyond the toe of her pretty boot before she suggested, "Well?"

"Oh, nothing! Only it got to be rather tiresome, toward the last."

"Why did you stay so long?"

"I couldn't get away; they wouldn't let me go. They kept proposing this and that, and then they wanted to arrange something for to-morrow. But I wouldn't."

"They are rather persistent," said Mrs. Meredith.

"Yes, they are persistent. But they are very kind — they are very good-natured. I wish — I wish I liked them better!"

"Don't you like them?"

"Oh, I like them, yes, in a kind of way. They're a very familyish sort of a family; they're so much bound up in one another. Of course they can do a

great many nice things : Miss Bloomingdale is really
wonderful with her music; and Josie sketches very
nicely; and Roberta sings beautifully, — there's no
denying it; but they don't talk very much, and they're
all so tall and handsome and blond; and they sit
round with their hands arranged in their laps, and
keep waiting for me to say things; and then their
mother starts them up and makes them do something.
The worst is she keeps dragging in Mr. Bloomingdale
all the time. There isn't anything that doesn't suggest him — what he thinks, what he says, where he's
been and what he did there; just how far he's got on
his way home by this time; how he's never seasick,
but he doesn't like rough weather. I began to dread
the introduction of a new subject: it was so sure to
bring round to him. Don't you think they're of rather
an old-fashioned taste ? "

"I never liked this family very much," said Mrs.
Meredith. "They seemed very estimable people, but
not — "

"Our kind ? No, decidedly. Did Dr. Olney stay
long ? "

"No. Why do you ask ? " Mrs. Meredith returned,
with a startled look.

"Oh, nothing. You seemed to be quite chummy
with him, and not to want me round a great deal when
I came in." Miss Aldgate had discovered the toe of
her boot just beyond her skirt, apparently with some
surprise, and she leaned forward to touch it with the
point of her parasol, as if to make sure of it. "Is he

coming again this evening?" she asked, leaning back in her chair, and twisting her parasol by its handle.

"Not unless I send for him. I have his sleeping medicine."

"Yes. And I know how to drop it. Did he think it strange my being away from you so much when you needed a doctor?"

"He knew I didn't need any doctor. Why do you ask such a question as that?"

"I don't know. I thought it might have struck him. But I thought I had better try and see if I could get used to them or not. They're pretty formal people — conventional. I mean in the way of dress and that kind of thing. They're formal in their ideals, don't you know. They would want to do just what they thought other people were doing; they would be dreadfully troubled if there was anything about them that was not just like everybody else. Do you think Mr. Bloomingdale would be so?"

"I never liked his family very much," Mrs. Meredith repeated. "What little I saw of them," she added, as if conscientiously.

"Oh, that doesn't count, Aunt Caroline!" said the girl, with a laugh. "You never liked the families of any of the Americans that you thought fancied me. But the question is not whether we like his family, but whether he's like them."

"You can't separate him from his family, Rhoda. You must remember that. Each of us is bound by a thousand mysterious ties to our kindred, our ancestors; we can't get away from them —"

"Oh, what stuff, aunty!" Miss Aldgate was still greatly amused. "I should like to know how I'm bound to my mother's family, that I never saw one of; or to her father or grandfather?"

"How?" Mrs. Meredith gasped.

"Yes. Or how much they were bound to me, if they never tried to find me out or make themselves known by any sort of sign? I'm bound to you because we've always been together, and I was bound to Uncle Meredith because he was good to me. But there isn't anything mysterious about it. And Mr. Bloomingdale is bound to his family in the same way. He's fond of them because he's been nice to them and they've been nice to him. I wonder," she mused, while Mrs. Meredith felt herself slowly recoil from the point which she had been suddenly caught up to, "whether I really care for him or not? There were very nice things about him; and no, he was not tiresome and formal-minded like them. I wish I had been a little in love with some one, and then I could tell. But I've never had anything but decided dislikings, though I didn't dislike *him* decidedly. No, I rather liked him. That is, I thought he was *good.* Yes, I respected his goodness. It's about the only thing in this world you *can* respect. But now, I remember, he seemed very young, and all the younger because he thought it was his duty as a minister to seem old. Did *you* care very much for his sermon?"

Rhoda came to the end of her thinking aloud with a question that she had to repeat before her aunt asked drearily in answer, "What sermon?"

"Why, we only heard him once! The one he preached in Florence. I didn't have a full sense of his youth till I heard that. Isn't it strange that there are ever young ministers? I suppose people think they can make up in inspiration what they lack in experience. But that day when I looked round at those men and women, some of them gray-haired, and most of them middle-aged, and all of them knowing so much more about life, and its trials and temptations, and troubles and sorrows, than poor Mr. Bloomingdale — I oughtn't to call him *poor* — and heard him going on about the birds and the flowers, I wondered how they could bear it. Of course it was all right; I know that. But if the preacher *shouldn't* happen to be inspired, wouldn't it be awful? How old do you suppose Dr. Olney is?"

"I don't know."

"He seems rather bald. Do you think he is forty?"

"Dear me, no, child! He isn't thirty yet, I dare say. Some men are bald much earlier than others. It's a matter of — heredity."

"Heredity! Everything's heredity with you, Aunt Caroline!" the girl laughed. "I'll bet he's worn it off by thinking too much in one particular spot. You know that they say now they can tell just what place in the brain a person thinks this or that; and just where the will-power comes from when you wink your eye, or wiggle your little finger. I wonder if Dr. Olney knows all those things? Have you tried him on your favorite heredity yet?"

"What do you mean, Rhoda?"

"I know you have!" the girl exulted. "Well, he is the kind of man I should always want to have for my doctor if I had to have one; though I don't think he's done you a great deal of good yet, Aunt Caroline: you look wretched, and I shall feel like scolding Dr. Olney when he comes again. But what I mean is, he has such noble ideas: don't you think he has?"

"Yes — yes. About what?"

"Why, about the negroes, you know." Mrs. Meredith winced at the word. "I never happened to see it in that light before. I thought when we had set them free, we had done everything. But I can see now we haven't. We do perfectly banish them, as far as we can; and we don't associate with them half as much as we do with the animals. I got to talking with the Bloomingdales this afternoon, and I had to take the negroes' part. Don't you think that was funny for a Southern girl?" Mrs. Meredith looked at her with a ghastly face, and moved her lips in answer, without making any sound. "They said that the negroes were an inferior race, and they never could associate with the whites because they never could be intellectually equal with them. I told them about that black English lawyer from Sierra Leone that talked so well at the *table d'hôte* in Venice — better than anybody else — but they wouldn't give way. They were very narrow-minded; or the mother was; the rest didn't say anything; only made exclamations. Mrs. Bloomingdale said Dr. Olney must be a

very strange physician, to have those ideas. I hope
Mr. Bloomingdale isn't like her. You would say he
was a good deal younger than Dr. Olney, wouldn't
you?"

"Yes — not so very. But why —"

Rhoda broke out into a laugh of humorous per-
plexity. "Why, if he were only a little older, or a
good deal older, he could advise me whether to marry
him or not?" The laughter faded suddenly from her
eyes, and she fell back dejectedly against her chair,
and remained looking at her aunt, as if trying to read
in her face the silent working of her thought. "Well?"
she demanded, finally.

Mrs. Meredith dropped her eyes. "Why need you
marry any one?"

"What a funny question!" the girl answered, with
the sparkle of a returning smile. "So as to have
somebody to take care of me in my old age!" The
young like to speak of age so, with a mocking in-
credulity; they feel that, however it may have fared
with all the race hitherto, they never can be old, and
they like to make a joke of the mere notion. "You'll
be getting old yourself some day, Aunt Caroline, and
then what shall I do? Don't you think that a woman
ought to get married?"

"Yes — yes. Not always — not necessarily. Certainly not to have some one to take care of her."

"Of course not! That would be a very base
motive. I suppose I really meant, have somebody
for *me* to take care of. I think that is what keeps

5

one from being lonesome more than anything else.   I
do feel so alone sometimes.   It seems to me there are
very few girls so perfectly isolated.   Why, just think!
With the exception of you, I don't believe I've got a
single relation in the world."   Rhoda seemed interested rather than distressed by the fact.   " Now there
are the Bloomingdales," she went on ; " it seems as if
they had connections everywhere.   That is something
like a family.   If I married Mr. Bloomingdale, I could
always have somebody to take care of as long as I
lived.   To be sure, they would be Bloomingdales,"
she added, dreamily.

"Rhoda!" said her aunt, "I cannot let you speak
so.   If you are in earnest about Mr. Bloomingdale —"

" I am.   But not about his family — or not so much
so."

"You cannot take him without taking his family ;
that is always the first thing to be thought of in marriage, and young people think of it the last.   The
family on each side counts almost as much as the
couple themselves in a marriage."

"Mine wouldn't," the girl interpolated.   "There's
so very little of it ! "

If Mrs. Meredith was trying to bring the talk to
this point, she now seemed to find herself too suddenly
confronted with it, and she shrank back a little.   "I
don't mean that family is the *first* thing."

"You just *said* it was, aunty ! "

"The first thing," Mrs. Meredith continued, ignoring the teasing little speech, "is to make sure of yourself, to be satisfied that you love *him*."

"It's so much easier," the girl sighed in mock-seriousness, "to be satisfied that I don't love *them*."

"But that won't do, Rhoda," said Mrs. Meredith, "and I can't let you treat the matter in this trivial spirit. It is a most important matter — far more important than you can realize."

"I can't realize anything about it — that's the trouble."

"You can realize whether you wish to accept him or not."

"No; that's just what I can't do."

"You've had time enough."

"I've had nearly a week. But I want all the time there is; it wouldn't be any too much. I must see him again — after seeing so much of his family."

"Rhoda!" her aunt called sternly to her from the sofa.

But Rhoda did not respond with any sort of intimidation. She was looking down into the street from the window where she sat, and she suddenly bowed. "It was Dr. Olney," she explained. "He was just coming into the hotel, and he looked up. I wonder how he knew it was our window? He seems twice as young with his hat on. I wish he'd wear his hat in the room. But of course he can't."

Everything that had happened since Rhoda came in made it more difficult for Mrs. Meredith to discharge the duty that she thought she had nerved herself up to. She had promised herself that if Rhoda had decided to accept Mr. Bloomingdale, she would speak,

and tell her everything; but she was not certain yet
that the girl had decided, though from the way in
which she played with the question, and her freedom
from all anxiety about it, she felt pretty sure that she
had. She wished, vaguely, perversely, weakly, that
she had not, for then the ordeal for them both could
be postponed indefinitely again. She sympathized
with the girl in her trials through the young minister's
family, who were so repugnant to her in their eagerness for her, and she burned with a prophetic indignation in imagining how such people would cast her off
when they knew what she really was. The young
man himself seemed kind and good, and if it were a
question of him alone, she believed she could trust
him; but these others! that mother, those sisters!
She recoiled from the duty of humiliating the poor
girl before them, so helplessly, innocently, ignorantly
guilty of her own origin. The child's gayety and
lightness, her elfish whimsicality and thoughtless
superficiality, as well as those gleams and glimpses of
a deeper nature which a word or action gave from
time to time, smote the elder woman's heart with a
nameless pain and a tender compassion. By all her
circumstance Rhoda had a right to be the somewhat
spoiled and teasing pretty thing that she was; and all
that sovereign young-ladyishness which sat so becom-
ingly upon her was proper to the station a beautiful
young girl holds in a world where she has had only to
choose and to command. But Mrs. Meredith shuddered to think with what contempt, open or masquerad-

ing as pity, all this would be denied to her. Doubtless she exaggerated; the world slowly changes; it condones many things to those who are well placed in it; and it might not have fared so ill with the child as the woman thought; but Mrs. Meredith had brooded so long upon her destiny that she could see it only in the gloomiest colors. She was darkling in its deepest shadow when she heard Rhoda saying, as if at the end of some speech that she had not caught, "But *he* doesn't seem to have any more family than I have."

"Who?" Mrs. Meredith asked.

"Dr. Olney."

"You don't know anything about his family."

"Well, I don't know anything about my own," Rhoda answered, lightly. She added, soberly, after a moment: "Don't you think it's rather strange that my mother's family never cared to look us up in any way? Even if they were opposed to her marrying papa, one would think they might have forgiven it by this time. The family ties are so strong among the French."

Mrs. Meredith dropped her eyes, and murmured, "It may be different with the Creoles."

"No, I don't believe it is. I've heard it's more so. Did papa never see any of mamma's family but her father? It seems so strange that she should have been as much alone as I am. I know I have *you*, Aunt Caroline. Well, I don't know what to think about Mr. Bloomingdale. I'm always summing up his virtues; he's very good, and he's good-looking,

and he's good-natured. He's rich, though I don't let
that count. He parts his hair too much on one side,
but that doesn't matter, I could make him part it in
the middle, and it's a very pretty shade of brown.
His eyes are good, and his mouth wouldn't be weak if
he wore his beard full. I think he has very good
ideas, and I'm sure he would be devoted all his days.
It isn't so easy to sum a person up, though, is it? I
wish I knew whether I cared for him. I don't believe
I've ever been in love with anybody yet. Of course,
I've had my fancies. I do respect Mr. Bloomingdale,
and when I think how very anxious he was to have
me care for him, I don't know but I could if I really
tried. But ought one to have to try? That's the question. Oughtn't the love to go of itself, without being
pushed or pulled? I wish I knew! Aunt Caroline,
do you believe in 'learning to love' your husband
after marriage? That's what happens in some of the
stories; but it seems very ridiculous. I wish it was
my *duty* to marry him — or not to; then I could decide. I believe I'm turning out quite a slave of duty.
I must have 'caught it' from you, Aunt Caroline.
Now I can imagine myself sacrificing anything to duty.
If Mr. Bloomingdale were to step ashore from the
next steamer, and drive to the hotel without stopping
to take breath, and get himself shown up here, and
say, 'I've just dropped in, Miss Aldgate, to offer you
the opportunity of uniting your life with mine in a
high and holy purpose — say working among the poor
on the east side in New York, or going down to edu-

Irony

cate the black race in the South ' — I believe I should
seize the opportunity without a murmur. Perhaps he
may. Do you think he will?"

Rhoda ended her monologue with a gay look at
her aunt, who was silent at the end, as she had been
throughout, turning the trouble before them over and
over in her mind. As happens when we are preoccupied with one thing, all other things seem to tend
toward it and bear upon it; half a dozen mere acci-
dents of the girl's spoken reverie touched the sore
place in Mrs. Meredith's soul and fretted it to an
anguish that she asked herself how she could bear. It
all accused and judged and condemned her, because
she had kept putting by the duty she had to discharge,
and making it contingent upon that decision of the
girl's which she was still far from ascertaining. In
her recoil from this duty she had believed that if it
need not be done at this time, it somehow need never
be done; or she had tried to believe this. If Rhoda
rejected this young man, she might keep her safe forever from the fact which she felt must wreck the life
of the light-hearted, high-spirited girl. That was the
refuge which Mrs. Meredith had taken from the task
which so strongly beset her; but when she had formulated the case to herself, the absurdity, the impossibil-
ity of her position appeared to her. If Rhoda cared
nothing for Mr. Bloomingdale, the day would come
when she would care everything for some one else;
and that day could not be postponed, nor the duty of
that day. It would be crueler to leave her unarmed

against the truth until the moment when her heart was set upon a love, and then strike her down with it. Mrs. Meredith now saw this; she saw that the doubt in which she was resting was the very moment of action for her; and that the occasion was divinely appointed for dealing more mercifully with the child than any other that could have offered. She had often imagined herself telling Rhoda what she had to tell, and with the romantic coloring from the novels she had read, she had painted herself in the heroic discharge of her duty at the instant when the girl was radiant in the possession of an accepted love, and had helped her to renounce, to suffer, and to triumph. She had always been very strong in these dramatized encounters, and had borne herself with a stony power throughout, against which the bruised and bleeding girl had rested her broken spirit; but now she cowered before her. She longed to fall upon her knees at her feet, and first implore her forgiveness for what she was going to do, and not speak till she had been forgiven; but habit is strong, really stronger than emotion of any sort, and so Mrs. Meredith remained lying on her sofa, and merely put up her fan to shut out the sight of the child, as she said, "And if it were your duty to give up Mr. Bloomingdale, could you do it?"

"Oh, instantly, Aunt Caroline!" answered Rhoda, with a gay burlesque of fortitude. "I would not hesitate a single week. But why do you ask such an awful question?"

"Is it a very awful question?" Mrs. Meredith palpitated.

"Well, rather! One may wish to give a person up, but not as a *duty*."

Mrs. Meredith understood this well enough, but it was her perfect intelligence concerning the whole situation that seemed to disable her. She made out to say, "Then you have decided not to give him up yet?"

"I've decided — I've decided — let me think! — not to decide till I see him again! What do you mean by if it were my duty to give him up?"

"It would be your duty," Mrs. Meredith faltered, "to give him up, unless you were sure you loved him."

"Oh, yes; certainly. *That.*"

"You wouldn't wish him, after you've seen so much of his family, not to know everything about yours, if you decided to accept him?"

"Why, you're all there is, Aunt Caroline! You're the end of the story. I should hope he understood that. What else is there?"

"Nothing — nothing — There is very little. But we ought to tell Mr. Bloomingdale all we know — of your mother's family."

"Why, certainly. I expected to do that. There was nothing disgraceful about them, I imagine, except their behavior toward mamma."

"No —"

"You speak as if there *were*. What are you keeping back, Aunt Caroline?" Rhoda sat upright, and faced her aunt with a sort of sudden fierceness which she sometimes showed when she was roused to self-assertion. This was seldom, in the succession of her amiable moods, but when it happened, Mrs. Meredith saw in it the outbreak of the ancestral savagery, and shuddered at it as a self-betrayal rather than a self-assertion; but perhaps self-assertion is this with all of us. " What are you hinting at? If there was anything dishonorable — "

Mrs. Meredith found herself launched at last. She could not go back now; she could not stop. She had only the choice, in going on, of telling the truth, or setting sail to shipwreck under some new lie. For this, both will and invention failed her; she was too weak mentally, if she was not too strong morally, for this. She went on, with a kind of mechanical force.

" If there were something dishonorable that was not their fault, that was their wrong, their sorrow, their burden — what should you think of your father's marrying your mother, with a full knowledge of it? "

" I should think he did nobly and bravely to marry her. But that's nothing. What was the disgrace? What had they done, that they had to suffer innocently? You needn't be afraid of telling me everything. I don't care what Mr. Bloomingdale or any one thinks; I shall be proud of them for it; I shall be glad! " Mrs. Meredith saw with terror that the girl's fancy had kindled with some romantic conjecture. " Who *was* my grandfather? "

" I know very little about him, Rhoda," said Mrs. Meredith, seeking to rest in this neutral truth. " Your father never told me much, except that he was a Creole, and — and rich ; and — and — respected, as those things went there, among his people — "

" Was he some old slaver, like those in Mr. Cable's book ? I shouldn't care for that ! But that would have been his fault, and it wouldn't have been any great disgrace ; and you said — And my grandmother — who was *she* ? "

" She was — not his wife."

" Oh ! " said the girl, with a quick breath, as if she had been struck over the heart. " *That* was how the dishonor — " She stopped, with an absent stare fixed upon her aunt, who waited in silence for her to realize this evil which was still so far short of the worst. Where she sat she could not see the blush of shame that gradually stained the girl's face to her throat and forehead. " *Who* was she ? "

 Mrs. Meredith tried to think how the words would sound as she said them, and simultaneously she said them, " She was his slave."

The girl was silent and motionless. With her head defined against the open window, her face showed quite black toward her aunt, as if the fact of her mother's race had remanded her to its primordial hue in touching her consciousness. Mrs. Meredith had risen, and sat with one hand grasping the wrap that still covered her feet, as if ready to cast it loose and fly her victim's presence, if it became intolerable. But she found herself too weak to stand up, and she waited, throbbing and quaking, for Rhoda to speak.

Black
Stereotype

The girl gave a little, low, faltering laugh, an inarticulate note of such pathetic fear and pitiful entreaty that it went through the woman's heart. "Aunt Caroline, are you crazy?"

"Crazy?" The word gave her an instant of strange respite. Was she really mad, and had she long dreamed this thing in the cloudy deliriums of a sick brain? The fact of her hopeless sanity repossessed her from this tricksy conjecture. If I were *only* crazy!"

"And you mean to say — to tell me — that — that — I am — *black?*"

"Oh, no, poor child! You are as white as I am — as any one. No one would ever think — "

"But I have that blood in me? It is the same thing!" An awful silence followed again, and then the girl said: "And you let me grow up thinking I was white, like other girls, when you knew — You let me pass myself off on myself and every one else, for what I wasn't! Oh, Aunt Caroline, what are you telling me this ghastly thing for? It *isn't* true! You couldn't have let me live on all these years thinking I was a white person, when — You would have told me from the very beginning, as soon as I could begin to understand anything. You wouldn't have told me all those things about my mother's family, and their being great people, and disowning her, and all that! If this is true you wouldn't have let me believe that, you and Uncle Meredith?"

"We let you believe it, but you made it up yourself; we never told you anything."

"But you couldn't have thought that was being
honest, and so you couldn't have done it — *you*
couldn't. And so it isn't any of it true that you've
just told me. But why did you tell me such a thing?
I don't believe you *have* told me it. Why, I must be
dreaming. It's as if — as if — you were to come to
a perfectly well person, and tell them that they were
going to die in half an hour. Don't you see? How
can you tell me such a thing? Don't you understand
that it tears my whole life up, and flings it out on the
ground? But you *know* it isn't true. Oh, my, I think
my head will burst! Why don't you speak to me, and
tell me why you said such a thing? Is it because you
don't want me to marry Mr. Bloomingdale? Well, I
won't marry him. *Now* will you say it?"

"Rhoda!" her aunt began, "whether you married
Mr. Bloomingdale or not, the time had come — "

"No! The time had gone. It had come as soon
as I could speak or understand the first word. Then
would have been the time for you to tell me such a
thing if it were true, so that I might have grown up
knowing it, and trying to bear it. But it isn't true,
and you're just saying it for some other reason. What
has happened to you, Aunt Caroline? I am going to
send for Dr. Olney; you're not well. It's something
in that medicine of his, I know it is. Let me look at
you!" She ran suddenly toward Mrs. Meredith, who
recoiled, crouching back into the corner of her sofa.
The girl broke into a hysterical laugh. "Do you
think I will hurt you? Oh, Aunt Caroline, take it

back, take it back! See, I'll get on my knees to
you!" She threw herself down before the sofa where
Mrs. Meredith crouched. "Oh, you *couldn't* have
been so wicked as to live such a lie as that!"

"It was a lie, the basest, the vilest," said Mrs. Meredith, with a sort of hopeless gasp. "But I never saw
the time when I *must* tell you the truth — and so I
couldn't."

"Oh, no, no! Don't take yourself from me!"
The girl dropped her head on the woman's knee, and
broke into a wild sobbing. "I don't know what you're
doing this for. It can't be true — it can't be real.
Shall I *never* wake from it, and have you back? You
were all I had in the world, and now, if you were not
what I thought you, so true and good, I haven't even
you any more. Oh, oh, oh!"

"Oh, it was all wrong," said Mrs. Meredith, in a
tearless misery, a dry pang of the heart for which her
words were no relief. "There hasn't been a day or
an hour when I haven't felt it; and I have always
prayed for light to see my duty, and strength to do it.
God knows that if I could bear this for you, how
gladly I would do it. I have borne it all these years,
and the guilt of the concealment besides; that is
something, though it is nothing to what you are suffering. I know that — I know that!"

The girl sobbed on and on, and the woman repeated
the same things over and over, a babble of words in
which there was no comfort, no help, but which suf-
ficed to tide them both over from the past which had

dropped into chaos behind them to a new present in which they must try to gain a footing once more.

The girl suddenly ceased to bemoan herself, and lifted her head, to look into her aunt's face. "And my mother," she said, ignoring the piteous sympathy she saw, "was she my *father's* slave, too?"

"She was your father's wife. Slavery was past then, and he was too good a man for anything else, though he knew his marriage would ruin him, as it did."

"At least there is *some* one I can honor, then; I can honor *him*," said the girl, with an unpitying hardness in her tone. She rose to her feet, and turned toward the door of her own room.

"Is there — is there anything else that I can tell — that you wish to know?" her aunt entreated. "Oh, child! If you could only understand —"

"I do understand," said the girl.

Mrs. Meredith, in her millionfold prefigurations of this moment, had often suffered from the necessity of insinuating to the ignorance of girlhood all the sad details of the social tragedy of which she was the victim. But she perceived that this at least was to be spared her, that the girl had somehow instantly realized the whole affair in these aspects. In middle life we often forget, amidst the accumulations of experience, how early the main bases of it were laid in our consciousness. We suppose, when we are experienced, that knowledge comes solely from experience; but knowledge, or if not knowledge, then truth, comes largely from perception, from instinct, from divination, from the intelligence of our mere potentialities. A man can be anything along the vast range from angel to devil; without living either the good thing or the bad thing in which his fancy dramatizes him, he can perceive it. His intelligence may want accuracy, though after-experience often startlingly verifies it; but it does not want truth. The materials of knowledge accumulate from innumerable unremembered sources. All at once, some vital interest precipitates the latent electricity of the cloudy mass in a flash that illumines the world with a shadowless brilliancy and shows everything in its very form and meaning. Then the witness perceives that somehow from the beginning of conscious being he had understood all this before, and every influence and circumstance had tended to the significance revealed.

The proud, pure girl who had been told that her mother was slave-born and sin-born, had lived as carefully sheltered from the guilt and shame that are in the world as tender love and pitying fear could keep her; but so much of the sad fact of evil had somehow reached her that she stood in a sudden glare of the reality. She understood, and she felt all scathed within by the intelligence, by whatever the cruelest foe could have told her with the most unsparing fulness, whatever the fondest friend could have wished her not to know. The swiftness of these mental processes no words can suggest; we can portray life, not living.

"I am going to my room, now," she said to her aunt, "and whatever happens, don't follow me, don't call me. If you are dying, don't speak to me. I have a right to be alone."

She crossed to the door of her chamber opening from the little parlor, and closed it behind her, and her aunt fell back again on her sofa. She was too weak to follow her if she had wished, and she was too wise to wish it. She lay there revolving the whole misery in her mind, turning it over and over ten thousand times. She said to herself that it was worse, far worse, than she had ever pictured it; but in fact it was better, for her. She pretended otherwise, but for her there was the relief in the situation of a lie owned, a truth spoken, and with whatever heart-wrung drops she told the throes of the anguish beyond that door, for herself she was glad. It was monstrous to be glad, she knew that; but she knew that she was glad.

After awhile she began to be afraid of the absolute silence that continued in Rhoda's room, and then she did what men would say a man would not have done; she crept to the door and peeped and listened. She could not hear anything, but she saw Rhoda sitting by the table writing. She went back to her sofa, and lay there more patiently now; but as the time passed she began to be hungry; with shame that did not suffer her to ring and ask for anything to eat, she began to feel the weak and self-pitiful craving of an invalid for food.

The time passed till the travelling-clock on the

6

mantel showed her that it was half-past seven. Then
Rhoda's door was flung open, and the girl stood before
her with her hat on, and dressed to go out. She had
a letter in her hand, and she said, with a mechanical
hardness, " I have written to him, and I am going out
with the letter. When I come back — "

" You can send your letter out," pleaded her aunt ;
she knew what the girl had written too well to ask.
" It's almost dark ; it's too late for you to be out on
the streets alone."

" Oh, what could happen to *me* ? " demanded Rhoda,
scornfully. " Or if some one insulted a colored girl,
what of it ? When I come back I will pack for you,
and in the morning we will start for New Orleans, and
try to find out my mother's family."

Her aunt said nothing to this, but she set herself
earnestly to plead with the girl not to go out. " It
will be dark, Rhoda, and you don't know the streets.
Indeed you mustn't go out. You haven't had any
dinner — For my sake — "

" For *your* sake ! " said Rhoda. She went on, as if
that were answer enough, " I have written to him that
all is over between us — it was, even before *this :* I
could never have married him — and that when he
arrives we shall be gone, and he must never try to see
me again. I've told you all that you could ask, Aunt
Caroline, and now there is one thing I want you to
answer me. Is there any one else who knows this ? "

" No, indeed, child ! " answered Mrs. Meredith instantly, and she thought for the instant that she was

telling the truth. "Not another living soul. No one ever knew but your uncle — "

"Be careful, Aunt Caroline," said the girl, coming up to her sofa, and looking gloomily down upon her. "You had better always tell me the truth, now. Have you told *no* one else ? "

"No one."

"Not Dr. Olney ? "

It was too late, now that Mrs. Meredith perceived her error. She could not draw back from it, and say that she had forgotten ; Rhoda would never believe that. She could only say, "No, not Dr. Olney."

 "Tell me the truth, if you expect ever to see me again, in this world or the next. Is it the truth? Swear it ! "

"It is the truth," said the poor woman, feeling this new and astonishing lie triply riveted upon her soul ; and she sank down upon the pillow from which she had partly lifted herself, and lay there as if crushed under the burden suddenly rolled back upon her.

"Then I forgive you," said the girl, stooping down to kiss her.

The woman pushed her feebly away. "Oh, I don't want your forgiveness, now," she whimpered, and she began to cry.

Rhoda made no answer, but turned and went out of the room.

Mrs. Meredith lay exhausted. She was no longer hungry, but she was weak for want of food. After a while she slid from the sofa, and then on her hands

and knees she crept to the table where the bottle that
held Dr. Olney's sleeping medicine stood.   She drank
it all off.   She felt the need of escaping from herself;
she did not believe it would kill her; but she must
escape at any risk.   So men die who mean to take
their lives; but it is not certain that death even is an
escape from ourselves.

VIII.

In the street where Rhoda found herself the gas
was already palely burning in the shops, and the
moony glare of an electric globe was invading the flush
of the sunset, whose after-glow still filled the summer
air in the western perspective. She did not know
where she was going, but she went that way, down the
slope of the slightly curving thoroughfare. She had
the letter which she meant to post in her hand, but
she passed the boxes on the lamp-posts without putting
it in. She no longer knew what else she meant to do,
in any sort, or what she desired; but out of the turmoil of horror, which she whirled round and round in,
some purpose that seemed at first exterior to herself
began to evolve. The street was one where she would
hardly have met ladies of the sort she had always supposed herself of; gentility fled it long ago, and the
houses that had once been middle-class houses had
fallen in the social scale to the grade of mechanics'
lodgings, and the shops, which had never been fashionable, were adapted strictly to the needs of a neighbor-
hood of poor and humble people. They were largely
provision stores, full of fruit, especially watermelons;
there were some groceries, and some pharmacies of
that professional neatness which pharmacies are of

everywhere. The roadway was at this hour pretty well deserted by the express wagons and butcher carts that bang through it in the earlier day; and the horse-cars coming and going on its incline and its final westward level, were in the unrestricted enjoyment of the company's monopoly of the best part of its space.

At the first corner Rhoda had to find her way through groups of intense-faced suburbans who were waiting for their respective cars, and who heaped themselves on board as these arrived, and hurried to find places, more from force of habit than from necessity, for the pressure of the evening travel was already over. When she had passed these groups she began to meet the proper life of the street — the women who had come out to cheapen the next day's provisions at the markets, the men, in the brief leisure that their day's work had left them before bedtime, lounging at the lattice doors of the drinking-shops, or standing listlessly about on the curb-stones smoking. Numbers of young fellows, of the sort whose leisure is day-long, exchanged the comfort of a mutual support with the house walls, and stared at her as she hurried by; and then she began to encounter in greater and greater number the colored people who descended to this popular promenade from the up-hill streets opening upon it. They politely made way for her, and at the first meeting that new agony of interest in them possessed her.

This was intensified by the deference they paid her as a young white lady, and the instant sense that she

New of
agony of
interest

had no right to it in that quality. She could have borne better to have them rude and even insolent; there was something in the way they turned their black eyes in their large disks of white upon her, like dogs, with a mute animal appeal in them, that seemed to claim her one of them, and to creep nearer and nearer and possess her in that late-found solidarity of race. She never knew before how hideous they were, with their flat wide-nostriled noses, their out-rolled thick lips, their mobile, bulging eyes set near together, their retreating chins and foreheads, and their smooth, shining skin; they seemed burlesques of humanity, worse than apes, because they were more like. But the men were not half so bad as the women, from the shrill-piped young girls, with their grotesque attempts at fashion, to the old grandmothers, wrinkled or obese, who came down the sloping sidewalks in their bare heads, out of the courts and alleys where they lived, to get the evening air. Impish black children swarmed on these uphill sidewalks, and played their games, with shrill cries racing back and forth, catching and escaping one another.

These colored folk were of all tints and types, from the comedy of the pure black to the closest tragical approach to white. She saw one girl, walking with a cloud of sable companions, who was as white as herself, and she wondered if she were of the same dilution of negro blood; she was laughing and chattering with the rest, and seemed to feel no difference, but to be pleased and flattered with the court paid her by the inky dandy who sauntered beside her.

all shades

"She has always known it; she has never felt it!"
she thought bitterly. "It is nothing; it is natural to
her; I might have been like her."

She began to calculate how many generations would
carry her back, or that girl back, in hue, to the black-
est of those loathsome old women. She knew what
an octoroon was, and she thought, "I am like her,
and my mother was darker, and my grandmother
darker, and my great-grander like a mulatto, and then
it was a horrible old negress, a savage stolen from
Africa, where she had been a cannibal."

A vision of palm-tree roofs and grass huts, as she
had seen them in pictures, with skulls grinning from
the eaves, floated before her eyes; then a desert with
a long coffle of captives passing by, and one black,
naked woman, fallen out from weakness, kneeling,
with manacled hands, and her head pulled back, and
the Arab slaver's knife at her throat. She walked
in a nightmare of these sights; all the horror of the
wrong by which she came to be, poured itself round
and over her.

She emerged from it at moments with a refusal to
accept the loss of her former self, like that of the
mutilated man who looks where his arm was, and cannot believe it gone. Like him, she had the full sense
of what was lost, the unbroken consciousness of what
was lopped away. At these moments all her pride re-
asserted itself; she wished to punish her aunt for
what she had made her suffer, to make her pay pang
for pang. Then the tide of reality overwhelmed her

again, and she grovelled in self-loathing and despair. From that she rose in a frenzy of longing to rid herself of this shame that was not hers; to tear out the stain; to spill it with the last drop of her blood upon the ground. By flamy impulses she thrilled towards the mastery of her misery through its open acknowledgment. She seemed to see herself and hear herself stopping some of these revolting creatures, the dreadfulest of them, and saying, "I am black, too. Take me home with you, and let me live with you, and be like you every way." She thought, "Perhaps I have relations among them. Yes, it must be. I will send to the hotel for my things, and I will live here in some dirty little back court, and try to find them out."

The emotions, densely pressing upon each other, the dramatizations that took place as simultaneously and insuccessively as the events of a dream, gave her a new measure of time; she compassed the experience of years in the seconds these sensations outnumbered.

All the while she seemed to be walking swiftly, flying forward; but the ground was uneven: it rose before her, and then suddenly fell. She felt her heart beat in the middle of her throat. Her head felt light, like the blowball of a dandelion. She wished to laugh. There seemed two selves of her, one that lived before that awful knowledge, and one that had lived as long since, and again a third that knew and pitied them both. She wondered at the same time if this were what people meant by saying one's brain was turned;

and she recalled the longing with which her aunt said, "If I were *only* crazy!" But she knew that her own exaltation was not madness, and she did not wish for escape that way. "There must be some other," she said to herself; "if I can find the courage for it, I can find the way. It's like a ghost: if I keep going towards it, it won't hurt me; I mustn't be afraid of it. Now, let me see! What *ought* I to do? Yes, that is the key: *Duty*." Then her thought flew passionately off. "If *she* had done her duty all this might have been helped. But it was her cowardice that made her murder me. Yes, she has killed me!"

The tears gushed into her eyes, and all the bitterness of her trial returned upon her, with a pressure of lead on her brain.

In the double consciousness of trouble she was as fully aware of everything about her as she was of the world of misery within her; and she knew that this had so far shown itself without that some of the passers were noticing her. She stopped, fearful of their notice, at the corner of the street she had come to, and turned about to confront an old colored woman, yellow like saffron, with the mild, sad face we often see in mulattoes of that type, and something peculiarly pitiful in the straight underlip of her appealing mouth, and the cast of her gentle eyes. The expression might have been merely physical, or it might have been an hereditary look, and no part of her own personality, but Rhoda felt safe in it.

"What street is this?" she asked, thinking suddenly, "She is the color of my grandmother; that is the way she looked;" but though she thought this she did not realize it, and she kept an imperious attitude towards the old woman.

"Charles Street, lady."

"Oh, yes; Charles. Where are all the people going?"

"The colored folks, lady?"

"Yes."

"Well, lady, they's a kyind of an evenin' meetin' at ouah choach to-night. Some of 'em's goin' there, I reckon; some of 'em's just out fo' a walk."

"Will you let me go with you?" Rhoda asked.

"Why, certainly, lady," said the old woman. She glanced up at Rhoda's face as the girl turned to accompany her. "But *I'm* a-goin' to choach."

"Yes, yes. That's what I mean. I want to go to your church with you. Are you from the South — Louisiana? She would be the color," she thought. "It might be my mother's own mother."

"No, lady: from Voginny. I was bawn a slave; and I lived there till after the wa'. Then I come Nawth."

"Oh," said Rhoda, disappointedly, for she had nerved herself to find this old woman her grandmother.

They walked on in silence for a while; then the old woman said, "I thought you wasn't very well, when I noticed you at the cawnah."

"I am well," Rhoda answered, feeling the tears

Colored church

start to her eyes again at the note of motherly kind-ness in the old woman's voice. "But I am in trouble; I am in trouble."

"Then you're gwine to the right place, lady," said the old woman, and she repeated solemnly these words of hope and promise which so many fainting hearts have stayed themselves upon: "'Come unto me, all ye that labor and are heavy laden, and I will give you rest unto your souls.' Them's the words, lady; the Lawd's own words. Glory be to God; glory be to God!" she added in a whisper.

"Yes, yes," said Rhoda, impatiently. "They are good words. But they are not for me. He can't make *my* burden light; He can't give *me* rest. If it were sin, He could; but it isn't sin; it's something worse than sin; more hopeless. If I were only a sin-ner, the vilest, the wickedest, how glad I should be!" Her heart uttered itself to this simple nature as freely as a child to its mother.

"Why, sholy, lady," said the old woman, with a little shrinking from her as if she had blasphemed, "sholy you's a sinnah?"

"No, I am not!" said the girl, with nervous sharp-ness. "If I were a sinner, my sins could be forgiven me, and I could go free of my burden. But nothing can ever lift it from me."

"The Lawd can do anything, the Bible says. He kin make the dead come to life. He done it oncet, too."

The girl turned abruptly on her. "Can He change your skin? Can He make black white?"

The old woman seemed daunted; she faltered. "I don't know as he ever tried, lady; the Bible don't tell." She added, more hopefully, "But I reckon He could do it if He wanted to."

"Then why doesn't He do it?" demanded the girl. "What does He leave you black for, when He could make you white?"

"I reckon He don't think it's worth while, if He can make me *willing to be black* so easy. Somebody's got to be black, and it might as well be me," said the old woman, with a meek sigh.

"No, no one need be black!" said Rhoda, with a vehemence that this submissive sigh awakened in her. "If He cared for us, no one would be!"

"Sh!" said the old woman, gently.

They had reached the church porch, and Rhoda found herself in the tide of black worshippers who were drifting in. The faces of some were supernaturally solemn, and these rolled their large-whited eyes rebukingly on the young girls showing all their teeth in the smiles that gashed them from ear to ear, and carrying on subdued flirtations with the polite young fellows escorting them. It was no doubt the best colored society, and it was bearing itself with propriety and self-respect in the court of the temple. If their natural gayety and lightness of heart moved their youth to the betrayal of their pleasure in each other in the presence of their Maker, He was perhaps propitiated by the gloom of their elders.

"'Tain't a regular evenin' meetin'," Rhoda's com-

panion explained to her.   It's a kind o' lecture." She
exchanged some stately courtesies of greeting with the
old men and women as they pushed into the church;
they called her sister, and they looked with at least
as little surprise and offence at the beautiful young
white lady with her as white Christians would have
shown a colored girl come to worship with them.
" De preacher's one o' the Southern students; I
ain't hud him speak; but I reckon the Lawd's sent
him, anyway."

Rhoda had no motive in being where she was except
to confront herself as fully and closely with the trouble
in her soul as she could.   She thought, so far as
such willing may be called thinking, that she could
strengthen herself for what she had henceforth to bear,
if she could concentrate and intensify the fact to her
outward perception; she wished densely to surround
herself with the blackness from which she had sprung,
and to reconcile herself to it, by realizing and owning
it with every sense.

She did not know what the speaker was talking
about at first, but phrases and words now and then
caught in her consciousness.   He was entirely black,
and he was dressed in black from head to foot, so that
he stood behind the pulpit light like a thick, soft
shadow cast upon the wall by an electric.   His absolute sable was relieved only by the white points of his
shirt-collar, and the glare of his spectacles, which, when
the light struck them, heightened the goblin effect of
his presence.   He had no discernible features, and

when he turned his profile in addressing those who sat at the sides, it was only a wavering blur against the wall. His voice was rich and tender, with those caressing notes in it which are the peculiar gift of his race.

The lecture opened with prayer and singing, and the lecturer took part in the singing; then he began to speak, and Rhoda's mind to wander, with her eyes, to the congregation. The prevailing blackness gave back the light here and there in the glint of a bald head, or from a patch of white wool, or the cast of a rolling eye. Inside of the bonnets of the elder women, and under the gay hats of the young girls, it was mostly lost in a characterless dark; but nearer by, Rhoda distinguished faces, sad, repulsive visages of a frog-like ugliness added to the repulsive black in all its shades, from the unalloyed brilliancy of the pure negro type to the pallid yellow of the quadroon, and these mixed bloods were more odious to her than the others, because she felt herself more akin to them; but they were all abhorrent. Some of the elder people made fervent responses to thoughts and sentiments in the lecture as if it had been a sermon. "That is so!" they said. "Bless the Lord, that's the truth!" and "Glory to God!" One old woman, who sat in the same line of pews with Rhoda, opened her mouth like a catfish, to emit these pious ejaculations.

The night was warm, and as the church filled, the musky exhalations of their bodies thickened the air,

and made the girl faint; it seemed to her that she
began to taste the odor; and these poor people, whom
their Creator has made so hideous by the standards of
all his other creatures, roused a cruel loathing in her,
which expressed itself in a frantic refusal of their
claim upon her. In her heart she cast them off with
vindictive hate. "Yes," she thought, "I should have
whipped them, too. They are animals; they are only
fit to be slaves." But when she shut her eyes, and
heard their wild, soft voices, her other senses were
holden, and she was rapt by the music from her
frenzy of abhorrence. In one of these suspenses,
while she sat listening to the sound of the lecturer's
voice, which now and then struck a plangent note,
like some rich, melancholy bell, a meaning began to
steal out of it to her whirling thoughts.

"Yes, my friends," it went on saying, "you got to
commence doing a person good if you expect to love
them as Jesus loved us when he died for us. And
oh, if our white brethren could only understand —
and they're gettin' to understand it — that if they
would help us a little more, they needn't hate us
so much, what a great thing," the lecturer lamely
concluded — "what a great thing it would be all
round!"

"Amen! Love's the thing," said the voice of the
old woman with the catfish mouth; and Rhoda, who
did not see her, did not shudder. Her response inspired the lecturer to go on. "I believe it's the one
way out of all the trouble in this world. You can't

fight your way out, and you can't steal your way out,
and you can't lie your way out. But you can *love*
your way out. And how can you love your way out?
By helpin' somebody else! Yes, that's it. Somebody
that needs your help. And now if there's any one
here that's in trouble, and wants to get out of trouble,
all he's got to do is to help somebody else out. Remember that when the collection is taken up durin'
the singin' of the hymn. Our college needs help, and
every person that helps our college helps himself.
Let us pray!"

The application was apt enough, and Rhoda did not
feel anything grotesque in it. She put into the plate
which the old woman passed to her from the collector
all the money she had in her purse, notes and silver,
and two or three gold pieces that had remained over
to her from her European travel. Her companion saw
them, and interrupted herself in her singing to say,
"The Lawd 'll bless it to you; He'll help them that
helps them that can't help themselves."

"Yes, that is the clew," the girl said to herself.
"That is the way out; the only way. I can endure
them if I can love them, and I shall love them if I try
to help them. This money will help them."

But she did not venture to look around at the
objects of her beneficence; she was afraid that the
sight of their faces would harden her heart against
them in spite of her giving, and she kept her eyes shut,
listening to their pathetic voices. She stood forgetful
after the lecturer had pronounced the benediction —
7

he was a   vinity student, and he could not forego
it — and her companion had to touch her arm.   Then
she started with a shiver, as if from a hypnotic
trance.

Once out on the street she was afraid, and begged
the old woman to go back to her hotel with her.

"Why, sholy, lady," she consented.

But Rhoda did not hear.   Her mind had begun
suddenly to fasten itself upon a single thought, a sole
purpose, and "Yes," she pondered, "that is the first
thing of all ; to forgive her ; to tell her that I forgive
her, and that I understand and pity her.   But how —
how shall I begin ?   I shall have to do her some good
to begin with, and how can I do that when I hate her
so ?   I do hate her ; I do hate her !   It is her
fault ! "

As she hurried along, almost running, and heedless
of the old woman at her side, trying to keep up with
her, it seemed to her that if her aunt had told her long
ago, when a child, what she was, she would somehow
not have been it now.

It was not with love, not with pardon, but with
frantic hate and accusal in her heart, that she burst
into the room, and rushed to Mrs. Meredith's sofa,
where she lay still.

"Aunt Caroline, wake up!   Can you sleep when
you see me going perfectly crazy?   It is no time for
sleeping!   Wake ! "

The moony pallor of an electric light suspended
over the street shone in through the naked window

and fell upon Mrs. Meredith's face. It was white, and as the girl started back her foot struck the empty bottle from which the woman had drained the sleeping medicine, and let lie where she had let it fall upon the floor. Rhoda caught it up, and flew with it to the light.

IX.

THE thing that had been lurking in a dark corner of Olney's mind, intangible if not wholly invisible, came out sensible to touch and sight when he parted with Mrs. Meredith. At first it masqueraded a little longer as resentment of that hapless creature's fate, a creature so pretty, so proud, and by all the rights of her youth and sex heiress of a prosperous and unclouded future, the best love and the tenderest care that any man could give her. Then it began to declare itself a fear lest the man whose avowal had given him the right to know everything concerning her, might prove superior to it, and nobly renounce his privilege, and gladly take her for what she had always seemed, for what, except in so remote degree, she really was. Then Olney knew that he was himself in love with her, and that he was judging a rival's possibilities by his own, and dreading them. He had an impulse to go back to Mrs. Meredith and say that he was ready to take all those risks and chances which she had counted so great, and laugh them to scorn in the gladness of his heart if he could only hope that Rhoda would ever love him. A few years before he would have obeyed his impulse, and even now he dramatized an obedience to it, and exacted from Mrs.

Meredith a promise that she would not speak to Miss Aldgate until he had found time to put his fortune to the touch, and if he won, would never speak to her. But at thirty he had his hesitations, his misgivings, not indeed as to the wish, but as to the way. For one thing, he was too late, if Mrs. Meredith's conjectures were right; and for another, he felt it dishonorable to do what he longed in his heart to do, and steal from this man, whom he began to hate, the love upon which his courageous wooing had given him the right to count. Such a thing would be not theft only in the possible but not probable case she did not care for his rival, and he had no means of knowing the fact as to that. It might be defended if not justified on the ground that he wished to keep her forever in ignorance of what it was Mrs. Meredith's clear duty otherwise to tell her; Olney comforted himself with the theory that a woman who had delayed in her duty so long would doubtless put it off till the last moment, and that until this Mr. Bloomingdale actually appeared, and there was no loop-hole left her, she would not cease attempting to escape from her duty.

He postponed any duty which he himself had in the matter through the love he now owned; he made it contingent upon hers; but all the same, he determined to forego no right it gave him. Again he had a mind to go back to Mrs. Meredith, and ask her to do nothing until Bloomingdale came, and then, before she spoke, to authorize him to approach the man as her family physician and deal tentatively, hypothetically, with the matter, and interpret his probable decision from his actual behavior.

This course, which appeared the only course open to him, commended itself more and more to Olney as he thought of it; here was something practicable, here was something that was perhaps even obligatory upon him; he tried to believe it was obligatory. But it occurred to him only after long turmoil of thinking and feeling in other directions, and it was half-past seven o'clock before he returned from a walk he took as a final means of clearing his mind, and went to Mrs. Meredith's room to propose it to her. He knocked several times without response, and then went to the office to see if she had gone out and left her key with the clerk; he was now in a hurry to speak to her.

The clerk felt in the pigeon-hole of Mrs. Meredith's number. "Her key isn't here, but that's no sign she hasn't gone out. Ladies seldom leave their keys when they go out; we're only too glad if they leave 'em when they go away for good. I thought she was sick."

"She would be able to drive out."

Olney mastered his impatience as well as he could, and went in to his dinner. After dinner he knocked again at Mrs. Meredith's door, and confirmed himself in the belief that she had gone out. After that it was not so easy to wait for her to come back. He wished to remain of the mind he had been about speaking to her of Rhoda, and to avow himself her lover at all risks, but more and more he began to feel that he was too late, that he was quixotic, that he was ridiculous. He felt himself wavering from his purpose, and he held to it all the more tenaciously for that reason. If he was willing to hazard all upon the chance of being in time, that gave him the right to ask that the girl might be spared; but when he thought she and Mrs. Meredith were probably spending the evening together with the Bloomingdales, his courage failed. It was but too imaginable that Miss Aldgate had made up her mind to accept that man, and that her aunt would tell her all that he longed to save her from knowing before he could prevent it.

When at last he went a third time to her door, he ventured to turn the knob, and the door opened to his inward pressure. It let in with him a glare of gas from the lamp in the entry, and by this light he saw Rhoda standing beside her aunt's sofa with the empty bottle in her hand. She had her hat on, and at the face she turned him across her shoulder, a shiver of prescience passed over him. It was the tragic mask, the inherited woe, unlit by a gleam of the brightness which had sometimes seemed Heaven's direct gift to the girl on whom that burden of ancestral sin and sorrow had descended.

"What is the matter?" he murmured.

Rhoda gave him the empty bottle. "She's drunk it all. She's dead."

"Oh, no," he almost laughed. "It would be too soon." He dropped on his knees beside the insensi-

3 selves

ble body, and satisfied himself by pulse and breath
that the life had not yet left it.   But to keep it there
was now the business, and Olney began his losing
fight with a sort of pluriscience in which it seemed to
him that he was multiplied into three selves : one ap-
plying all the antidotes and using all the professional
skill with instant coolness ;   another guarding the
probable suicide from the conjecture of the hotel
servants and keeping the whole affair as silent as possible ; another devotedly vigilant of the poor girl who
was so deeply concerned in the small chances of success
perceptible to Olney, and who, whether he succeeded
or not, was destined to so sad an orphanage.   When
he thought of the chance that fate was invisibly offer-
ing her, he almost wished he might fail, but he fought
his battle through with relentless scientific conscience.
At the end it was his part to say, " It's over ; she's
dead."

"I knew she was," Rhoda answered apathetically.
"I expected it."

"Where were you ? " he asked, with the sort of sad
futility with which, when all is done, the spirit con-
tinues its endeavor.   "Was she alone ? "

"Yes.   I had gone out," Rhoda said.

"What time was that ? "   Olney wondered that he
had not asked this before ; perhaps he had made some
mistake through not having verified the moment.

"It was about half-past seven," answered the girl.

"You went out at half-past seven !   And when did
you return ? "

"We had a quarrel. I didn't come back till nearly ten — when you came in."

The poignancy of Olney's interest remained, but it took another direction. "You were out all the evening *alone*? Excuse my asking," he made haste to add, "But I don't understand — "

"I wasn't alone," said Rhoda. "I met an old colored woman on the street, and she went with me to the colored church. She came home with me." The girl said this quietly, as if there were nothing at all strange in it.

Her calm left Olney in the question which he was always pressing home to himself; whether her aunt had told her that thing. It was on his tongue to ask her why she went to the colored church, and what her quarrel with her aunt was about. He asked her instead, "Did you think, when you left her, that Mrs. Meredith seemed different at all — that — ? "

"I didn't notice," said Rhoda. "No. She seemed as she often did. But I know she thought she hadn't taken enough of the medicine. She wanted to sleep more."

Rhoda sat by the window of the little parlor where she had sat when the dead woman had told her that dreadful thing, and she remembered how she had glanced out of it and seen Olney in the street. The gas was now at full blaze in the room, but she glanced through the window again, and saw that the day was beginning to come outside. She turned from the chill of its pale light, and looked at Olney. Through the irresistible association of ideas, she looked for his baldness with the lack-lustre eyes she lifted to his face.

"Is there anything you wish me — anything I can do?" he asked, after a silence, in which he got back to the level of practical affairs, though still stupefied from what Rhoda had said.

"No."

"I mean, notify your friends — your family — telegraph —"

"I have no friends — no relatives. We were alone; all our family are dead."

"But Mr. Meredith's family — there is surely some one that you can call upon at this time."

A strong compassion swelled in Olney's heart; he yearned to take her in his arms and be all the world to one who had no one in all the world.

She remained as if dazed, and then she said, with a perplexed look: "I was trying to think who there was. Mr. Meredith's people lived in St. Louis; I remember some of them when I was little. Perhaps my aunt would have their address."

She went into the adjoining chamber where the dead woman lay, in the atmosphere of useless drugs and effectless antidotes, and Olney thought, "It's the mechanical operation of custom; she's going to ask her," but Rhoda came back with an address-book in her hand, as if she had gone directly to Mrs. Meredith's writing case for it with no such error of cerebration.

"Here it is," she said.

"Very well. I'll telegraph them at once. But in the mean time, what will you do, Miss Aldgate? You can't stay here in the hotel — *she* can't. How can I be of use to you?" Olney felt all the disinterestedness in the world in asking, but in what he asked next he had a distinct consciousness of self-interest, or at least of selfish curiosity. "Shall I let your friends at the Vendome — "

"Oh, no, no, no!" she broke out. "Not on any account! I couldn't bear to see them. Don't think of such a thing! No, *indeed*, I can't let you!"

The self-seeker is never fully rewarded, and Olney was left with a doubt whether this reluctance meant abhorrence of the Bloomingdales, or unwillingness to receive kindness from them which might involve some loss of her perfect independence to the spirited girl; she would not choose or be chosen for any reason but one. He could not make out from her manner as yet whether her aunt had spoken what was on her mind to speak or not; it seemed such a cruel invasion of her rights even to conjecture, that he tried to put the question out of his thoughts.

He began again while he was sensible of an unequal struggle with the question, which intruded itself in the swift whirl of his anxieties, as to what could immediately be done for her.

"Is there anything else you would suggest?"

"No," said the girl, in the dreamy quiet she seemed helpless to emerge from. "I suppose it wouldn't do, even if we could find her. I was thinking of the old woman I saw to-night," she explained. "I would like to go and stay with her if I could."

"Is it some one you know?"

"No, I don't know her. I just met her on the street, and we went to the colored people's church together. I went out after dinner and left my aunt alone. That was when she drank it."

She added the vague sentences together with a child's heedlessness as to their reaching her listener's intelligence, and she did not persist in her whimsical suggestion.

Olney left it too. "You must let me get you another room," he said; "You can't stay here any longer," and he made her take her hat and come with him to the hotel parlor. He went to arrange the business with the clerk, and to tell him of Mrs. Meredith's death; then he had to go about other duties connected with the case, which he rather welcomed as a distraction; to notify the fact and cause of Mrs. Meredith's death to the authorities, and to give the funeral preparations in charge. But when this was all done, and he could no longer play off the aggregate of these minor cares against his great one, he began to be harassed again about Miss Aldgate.

X.

It was so much easier to dispose of the friendless
dead than the friendless living, Olney thought, with
a sardonic perception of one of the bitterest truths
in the world; and he was not consoled by the reflec-
tion that it is often the man readiest to do all for a
woman who can do nothing for her. At the same time
he hurried along imagining a scene in which Rhoda
owned her love for him, and for his sake and her own,
consented to throw convention to the winds, and to
unite her fate with his in a marriage truly solemnized
by the presence of death. He was aroused from this
preposterous melodrama by a voice that said, with
liking and astonishment, " Why, Dr. Olney!" and he
found himself confronted with Mrs. Atherton, whom
he had known as Miss Clara Kingsbury. In another
moment she had flooded him with inquiry and explanation, from which he emerged with the dim consciousness that he had told her how he happened not to be
in Florence, and had heard how she happened to be in
Boston. Her presence in the city at such an untimely
season was to be accounted for by the eccentric spirit
in which she carried on her visiting for the Associated
Charities; she visited her families in the summer,
while most people looked after their families only in

the winter. She excused herself by saying that Beverly was so near, and sometimes it gave her a chance for a little bohemian lunch with Mr. Atherton.

Olney laid his trouble before her. He knew from of old that if he could not count upon her tact, he could count upon her imagination, and he was quite prepared for the sympathy with which she rushed to his succor, a sympathy that in spite of the circumstances could not be called less than jubilant.

"Why, the poor, forlorn, little helpless creature!" she exulted. "I'll go to the hotel at once with you, doctor; and she must come down to Beverly with me, and stay till her friends come on for her."

The question whether he was not bound in honor to tell Mrs. Atherton just what Miss Aldgate was, crazily visited him, and became a kind of longing before he could rid himself of it; he dismissed it only upon the terms of a self-promise to entertain it some other time; and he availed himself of her good offices almost as joyfully as she proposed them. He had to submit to the romantic supposition which he was aware Mrs. Atherton was keeping out of her words and looks, and he joined her in the conspicuous pretence she made throughout the affair that he was acting from the most disinterested, the most scientific motives.

It was not so hard as he had fancied it might be to get Miss Aldgate's consent to Mrs. Atherton's hospitality. It was the only possible thing for her, and she acquiesced simply, like one accustomed to favors; she expressed a sense of the kindness done her, with a delicate self-respect which Olney hardly knew how to account for upon the theory that Mrs. Meredith had spoken to her. Apparently she appreciated all the necessities of the case, and she did not troublesomely interpose any of the reluctances of grief which he had expected. If he could have wished any difference in her it would have been for rather less composure; but then this might have been the apathy following the great shock she had received. He willingly accepted Mrs. Atherton's theory, hurriedly whispered at parting, that she did not realize what had happened yet; Mrs. Atherton seemed to prize her the more for it.

He came back from seeing them off on the train to the hotel, where he found a telegram from Mrs. Meredith's connections in St. Louis. They were very sorry; they were unable to come on; they would write. Olney felt a grateful lift of the heart in thinking of Miss Aldgate in Mrs. Atherton's affectionate keeping, as he crumpled the despatch in his hand and tossed it on his dismal white-marble hearth. He believed that he read between its words a revelation of the fact that the dead woman's husband had not kept Rhoda's secret from his family, and that these unable friends, whatever they wrote, were not likely to urge any claim to comfort the girl.

It was Mrs. Bloomingdale who came to do this with several of her large and passive daughters, about as long after the evening papers came out as would take her to drive over from the Vendome. Olney had been able to persuade the reporters who got hold of the case that there was nothing to work up in it, and the paragraph that Mrs. Bloomingdale saw was discreet enough; it attributed Mrs. Meredith's death to an overdose of the soporific prescribed for her, and it connected Olney's name with the matter as the physician who happened to be stopping in the hotel with the unfortunate lady.

"I came the instant I read it," Mrs. Bloomingdale explained, "for I couldn't believe the evidence of my senses," and she added such a circumstantial statement of her mental struggle with the fact projected into her consciousness as could leave no doubt that the fact itself was far less important than the effect produced upon her.

As Olney listened he lost entirely a lurking discomfort he had felt at Miss Aldgate's refusal to let those people have anything to do with her or for her in her calamity. Whatever the son might be, the mother was a vulgarly selfish woman, posing before him as a generous benefactress, who was also a martyr. "I asked for you, doctor," she went on, at the end of her personal history in connection with the affair, "because I preferred not to intrude upon that poor young creature without learning just how I ought to approach her. As I said to my daughter Roberta, in coming along" — she put the tallest and serenest of the big, still blondes in evidence with a wave of her hand — "I would be ruled entirely by what you said of the newspaper report."

Olney said of it dryly that it was quite correct.

"Oh, I am *so* relieved, doctor!" said Mrs. Bloomingdale. "I didn't know, don't you know — I thought perhaps that there were facts — details which you preferred to keep from the public; that there were peculiar circumstances — aberration, don't you know; and that kind of thing. But I'm so glad there wasn't!"

Olney felt a malicious desire to disturb this crowing complacency which he believed was the cover of mean anxieties and suspicions. He asked, "Do you mean suicide?"

"Well, no; not that exactly. But —" She stopped, and he merely said:

"There was no evidence of suicidal intent."

"Oh!" said Mrs. Bloomingdale, but, as he intended, not so crowingly this time. "And then — you think I can ask for Miss Aldgate?"

"Miss Aldgate is not here —" Olney began.

"Not here!"

"She is with Mrs. Atherton, at Beverly. She couldn't remain here, you know."

"And may I ask — do I understand — Why didn't Miss Aldgate let *us* know?"

Olney rejoiced to be able to say, "I suggested that, but she preferred not to disturb you."

"And *why* did she prefer that?" said Mrs. Bloomingdale, with rising crest.

"I'm sorry, I don't know. It was by accident that I met Mrs. Atherton on the street; she is a well-known lady here, and she at once took Miss Aldgate home with her."

8

At the bottom of his heart Olney did not feel altogether easy at what he knew of Miss Aldgate's relations to the Bloomingdale family. He would have liked to blind himself to facts that proved her weak or at least light-mindedly fond of any present pleasure at the cost of any future complication, but he was not quite able to do so, much as he wished to inculpate the Bloomingdales. He was silent, and attempted no farther explanation or defence of Rhoda's refusal to see them.

"I presume, Dr. Olney," Mrs. Bloomingdale went on, "that you know nothing of the circumstances of our acquaintance with Miss Aldgate; and I can't expect you to sympathize with my — my — surprise that she should have turned from us at such a time. But I must say that I am very greatly surprised. Or not surprised, exactly. Pained."

"I am very sorry," Olney said again. "I have no right to intervene in any matter so far beyond my functions as Mrs. Meredith's physician, but I venture to suggest that the blow which has fallen on Miss Aldgate is enough to account for what seems strange to you in —"

"Of course. Certainly. I make allowance for that," said Mrs. Bloomingdale; and Olney was aware of receiving this proof of her amiability, her liberality, with regret; he would have so willingly had it otherwise, in justification of Miss Aldgate. "And I know that the past year has been one of great anxiety both to Mrs. Meredith and Miss Aldgate. You knew they had lost their money?"

"No," said Olney, with a joyful throb of the heart, "I didn't."

"I have understood so. Miss Aldgate will be left without anything—in a manner. But that would have made no difference to us. We should have been only too glad to prove to her that it made no difference. But if she prefers not to see us— We expect my son by Wednesday's steamer in New York." She added this suddenly and with apparent irrelevance, but Olney perceived that she wished to test his knowledge of the whole case, and she had instantly learned from his face that he knew much more than he would own. But he made no verbal concession to her curiosity. "I think you met my son in Florence?" she said.

"I saw him at Professor Garofalo's one night."

"He was there a great deal. It was there he met — Mrs. Meredith." Olney said nothing, and Mrs. Bloomingdale rose, and as with the same motion her large daughters rose. "May I ask, Dr. Olney, that you will give Miss Aldgate our love, and say to her that if there is anything we can do, we shall be so — I suppose you have had to communicate with Mrs. Meredith's — or Mr. Meredith's rather — family?"

"Yes."

"They will be at the funeral, of course; and if —"

"They are not coming," said Olney. "They have telegraphed that they are unable to come."

"Oh," said Mrs. Bloomingdale; and after a little pause she said, "Good-afternoon," and led her girls out.

Olney felt that he had parted with an enemy, and
that though he had in one sort tried to keep a con-
scientious neutrality, he had discharged himself of an
offensive office in a hostile manner, that he had made
her his enemy if not Miss Aldgate's enemy. She sus-
pected him, he knew that, of having somehow come
between her and Miss Aldgate of his own will as well
as Rhoda's. In view of this fact he had to ask himself to be very explicit as to his feelings, his hopes,
his intentions; and after a season of close question,
the response was very clear. He could not doubt
what he wished to do; the only doubt he had was as
to how and where and whether he could do it.

XI.

THE day of the funeral Bloomingdale arrived. None of his family had come to the last rites, though Olney had made it a point both of conscience and of honor to let them know when and where the ceremony would take place. He felt that their absence was an expression of resentment, but that it was a provisional resentment merely. There was a terrible provisionality about the whole business, beginning with the provisional deposition of the dead in the receiving-vault at Mount Auburn, till it could be decided where the long-tormented clay was finally to rest. Every decision concerning the affair seemed postponed, but he did not know till when; death had apparently decided nothing; he did not see how life should.

Bloomingdale came to see him in the evening, after dinner. His steamer had been late in getting up to her dock, and he had missed the first train on to Boston. He explained the fact briefly to Olney, and he said he had come directly to see him. He recalled their former meeting in Florence, but said, with somehow an effect of disappointment, that he had taken an older man whom he had seen at Professor Garofalo's for Dr. Olney. On his part, Olney could have owned to an equal disappointment. He remembered perfectly that Mr. Bloomingdale was a slight, dark man; but the composite Bloomingdale type, from the successive impressions of his mother's and sisters' style, was so deeply stamped in his consciousness that he was surprised to find the young minister himself neither large nor blond. His mind wandered from him to the father whom he had never seen, but who had left so distinct a record of himself in his son, and not in his daughters, as fathers are supposed usually to do. Then Olney's thoughts turned to that whole vexed question of heredity, and he lost himself deeply in conjecture of Rhoda's ancestry, while Bloomingdale was feeling his way forward to inquire about her through explanation and interest concerning Mrs. Meredith, and a fit sympathy, a most intelligent and delicate appreciation of the situation in all its details. Before the fact formulated itself in his mind, Olney was aware of feeling that this man was as different from his family in the most essential and characteristic qualities as he was different from them in temperament and complexion.

"And now about Miss Aldgate, Dr. Olney," he said, with a kind of authority, which Olney instinctively, however unwillingly, admitted. "I shall have to tell you why I am so very anxious to know how she is — how she bears this blow. I am afraid my mother betrayed to you the hurt which she felt, that Miss Aldgate should not have turned to her in her trouble; but I can understand how impossible it was she should. Without reflecting upon my mother at all for her feeling — for I can see how she would feel as she does — I must say I don't share it. While Miss Aldgate was still uncertain about — about myself — it was simply impossible that she should receive any sort of favor or kindness from my family even in such an exigency as this. It would have been indelicate; it must have been infinitely easier for her to accept the good offices of a total stranger, as she has done. Dr. Olney, I have to ask *your* good offices — and I have first to make you a confidence, as my reason for asking them. I'm *sure* you will understand me!"

In the fervor of his feeling the young man's voice trembled, and Olney felt himself moved with a curious involuntary kindness for him — the sort of admiring pity which men have been said to feel toward a brave foeman they mean to fight to the death. "I had a very great hope — and I think I had grounds for my hope — that Miss Aldgate would have consented to be my wife when she met me, if this terrible visitation — if all had gone well." The words sent a cold thrill through Olney's heart, and the mere suggestion that Rhoda could be anybody's wife but his own steeled it against this pretender to her love. "I offered myself to her in Liverpool before she sailed, and she was to have given me her answer here when we met. Now, I don't know what to do. I don't know anything. The whole world seems tumbled back into chaos. I can't urge anything upon her at such a time. I'm not even sure that I can decently ask to see her. And yet if I don't, what may not she think? Can't you help me in this matter? You were Mrs. Meredith's physician, and you stand in a sort of relation to Miss Aldgate that would authorize you to let her know that I am here, and very anxious to know what her wish — her will — is as to our meeting. It might not be professional, exactly, but — I came to you with the hope that it might be possible. Does it seem asking too much? I should be very sorry — "

Olney saw that the man's sensitiveness was taking fire, and in spite of his resentment of a request which set aside all his own secret hopes and intentions as non-existent, he could not forbear a concession to his unwitting rival's generous feeling. "Not at all," he said; "but I doubt my authority to intervene in any way. I have no right — "

"Only the right I've suggested," the young man urged. "I wouldn't have you assume anything for my sake. But I know that the circumstances are more than ordinarily distressing, and that Mrs. Meredith's death came in a way that might make Miss Aldgate afraid that — that — there might be some shadow of change in me on account of them. At such times we have misgivings about everybody; but I wish it to be understood that *no* circumstance could influence my feeling toward her."

"I don't know whether I understand you exactly," said Olney, with a growing dread of the man's generosity.

"Why, I suppose, from what I am able to learn, that poor Mrs. Meredith committed suicide."

"Not at all," Olney promptly returned. "There is
no evidence of that. There's every indication that she
simply took an overdose of the medicine I prescribed.
It wouldn't have killed her of itself, but her forces
were otherwise weakened."

"I'm glad, for her sake, to hear it," said Bloomingdale, "but it would have made no difference with me
if it had been different. If she had taken her life in
a fit of insanity, as I inferred, it would only have made
me more constant in the feeling. There is no con-
ceivable disadvantage which would not have endeared
Miss Aldgate more to me. I could almost wish for
the direst misfortune, the deepest disgrace," he went
on, while the tears sprang to his eyes, "to befall her,
if only that I might show her that it counted nothing
against her, that it counted everything for her!"

Olney's heart sank within him, and he felt guilty
before this unselfish frankness, which, if a little boy-
ish, was still so noble. He knew very well that if
such a lover could be told everything, it would not
matter the least to him; that the girl might be as
black as ebony, and his passion would paint her divinely fairer than the lily. Olney knew this from his
own thoughts as well as from the other's words; he
was himself like the spirit he conceived:

"Du gleichst dem Geist dem du begreifst."

But he was aware of an instant purpose not to let his
rival be brought to the test; and he was aware at the
same time of a duty he had to let him somehow have

his chance. "After all," he reflected, "what reason have I to suppose that she ever cared a moment for me, or ever could care? Very likely she likes this fellow; he is lovable; he is a fine fellow, though I hate him so; and what right have I to stand between them? He must have his chance." When he came to this point, he said aloud, coldly, "I don't understand what you expect me to do."

"Nothing! Only this: to let me go and see the lady with whom Miss Aldgate is staying, and learn from her whether and when Miss Aldgate will see me. That's all I can reasonably ask. I ought to ask as much if I meant to give her up — and it's all that I ask meaning never to give her up. Yes, that's all I can ask!" he repeated, desperately.

"That will be a very simple matter," said Olney. "Miss Aldgate is with Mrs. Atherton, at Beverly. I can give you her address, and my card to her."

"Yes, yes! Thank you — thank you ever so much. But — but if I present myself without explanation, what will this lady think?"

"She'll give your name to Miss Aldgate, and that will be explanation enough," said Olney, finding something a little superfine in this hesitation, and refusing to himself to be the bearer of any sort of confidences to Mrs. Atherton, who would be only too likely to take a romantic interest in the devoted young minister. Olney meant to give him an even chance, but nothing more.

"True!" said Bloomingdale, nervously gnawing his

lip. "True!" He drew a long breath, and added, "Of course, I can't go now till morning."

Olney said nothing as to this. He was writing on his card Mrs. Atherton's address and the introduction for Bloomingdale which he combined with it. He had resolved to go down himself that night. Bloomingdale clung fervently to his hand in parting.

"I can never thank you enough!" he palpitated.

"You have very little to thank me for," said Olney.

XII.

IF Mrs. Atherton thought it strange of Dr. Olney to drive up to her sea-side door at half-past nine, out of a white fog that her hospitable hall lamp could pierce only a few paces down the roadway, she dissembled her surprise so well that he felt he was doing the most natural thing, not to say the most conventional thing, in the world. She was notoriously a woman of no tact, but of so much heart that where it was a question at once of friendship and of romance, as the question of Dr. Olney and of Miss Aldgate was with her, she exercised a sort of inspiration in dealing with it. She put herself so wholly at the service of their imagined exigency that she now made Olney feel his welcome most keenly: a welcome which expressed that she would have been equally glad and equally ready to receive him in her sweet-matted, warm-rugged, hearth-fire-lit little drawing-room, if he had suddenly appeared at half-past two in the morning. The Japanese portière had not ceased tinkling behind him when she appeared through it, with outstretched hand. She promptly refused his excuses. " I really believe I was somehow expecting you to-night; and I'm ashamed that Mr. Atherton isn't up to bear witness to my pre-sentiment. But he's had rather a tiresome day, in town, and he's gone to bed early. I'm glad to say that Miss Aldgate has gone to her room, too. She's feeling the reaction from the tension she's been in, and I hope it will be a complete letting down for her. Have you heard anything more from those strange people? Very odd they shouldn't any of them have come on!"

Mrs. Atherton meant the St. Louis connections of Mrs. Meredith, and Olney said, with an embarrassed frown, " No, they haven't made any sign yet."

" The strange thing about a tragedy of this kind is," Mrs. Atherton remarked, " that you never can realize that it's ended. You always think there's going to be something more of it. I suppose I was thinking that you had heard something disagreeable from those people, though I don't know what they could say or do to heighten the tragedy."

" I don't either," Olney answered. " But something else has happened, Mrs. Atherton. You were quite right in your foreboding that the end was not yet." He paused with a gloomier air than he knew, for Bloomingdale's appearance was to him by far the most tragical phase of the affair. Then he went on thoughtfully : " I hardly know how to approach the matter without seeming to meddle in it more than I mean to do. I wish absolutely to put myself outside of it. But there's a kind of necessity that I should tell you about it." As he said this the kind of necessity that he had thought there was instantly vanished, and left him feeling rather blank. There was no necessity at all that he should tell Mrs. Atherton what relation Bloomingdale bore, and wished to bear, toward Miss Aldgate. All that he had to do, if he had to do anything, was to tell her that he had given him his card to her, and that she might expect him in the morning, and so leave her to her conjectures. If he went beyond this, he must go very far beyond it, and not make any confidence for Bloomingdale without making a much ampler confidence for himself. "The fact is, I wish to submit a little case of conscience to you."

Mrs. Atherton was delighted; and if she had been drowsy before, this would have aroused her to the most vigilant alertness. She knew that the case of conscience must somehow have something to do with Miss Aldgate; she believed that it was nothing but a love affair in disguise, and a love affair, with a strong infusion of moral question in it, promised a pleasure to Mrs. Atherton's sympathetic nature which nothing else could give. "Yes?" she said.

"Mrs. Atherton," Olney resumed, "how far do you think a man is justified in pursuing an advantage which another has put in his hands unknowingly — say that another, who did not know that I was his enemy, had put in *my* hands?"

"Not very far, Dr. Olney," she answered, promptly. "In fact, not at all. That is, you might justify such a man, if the case were some one else's. But you couldn't justify him if the case were yours."

"I was afraid you would say so; I knew you would

say so. Well, the case is mine," said Olney, "and it's this. I've run down here to-night to tell you that I've given my card to a gentleman who will call here in the morning."

Olney paused, and Mrs. Atherton said, "I'm sure I shall be glad to see any friend of yours, Dr. Olney."

" He isn't my friend," Olney returned, gloomily.

" Then, any enemy," Mrs. Atherton suggested.

Olney put the little pleasantry by. " The day before Mrs. Meredith died, she told me something that I need not speak of except as it relates to this Mr. Bloomingdale."

" It's Mr. Bloomingdale who's coming, then ? "

" Yes. Do you know anything about him ? "

" Oh, no ! Only it's a very floral kind of name."

" I wish I could be light about the kind of person he is. But I can't. He's a very formidable kind of person : very sensible, very frank, very generous."

Mrs. Atherton shook her head with a subtle intelligence. " Those might be very disheartening traits — in another."

" They are. They complicate the business for me. This Mr. Bloomingdale has offered himself to Miss Aldgate." Mrs. Atherton's attentive gaze expressed no surprise ; probably she had divined this from the beginning. " He was to have had his answer when he met her in Boston," Olney said, with an effect of finding the words a bad taste in his mouth. " That was the arrangement in Liverpool. But, of course, now — "

He stopped, and Mrs. Atherton took the word, with a lofty courage:

"Of course now he has all the greater right to it."

"Yes," said Olney, though he did not see why.

"I shall be glad to see Mr. Bloomingdale when he comes," Mrs. Atherton went on; "and though it's an embarrassing moment, I must manage to prepare Miss Aldgate for his coming. She will certainly have her mind made up by this time."

There was something definitive in Mrs. Atherton's tone that made Olney feel as if he had transacted his business, and he rose. He had felt that he ought to tell Mrs. Atherton of his own hopes or purposes in regard to Miss Aldgate; but now that he had given Bloomingdale away, this did not seem necessary. In fact, by a sudden light that flashed upon it, he perceived that it would be allowing his rival a fairer chance if he let him have it without competition. Afterwards when he got out of the house he thought he was a fool to do this; but he could not go back and make his confession without appearing a greater fool; and he kept on to the station, and waited there till the last train for town came lagging along, and then he put himself beyond temptation, at least for the night.

He spent what was left of it in imaginary interviews, now with Mrs. Atherton, now with Bloomingdale, now with Rhoda, and now with all of them in various combinations, and constructed futures varying in character from the gayest happiness to the gloom of the

darkest tragedy, lit by the one high star of self-renun-
ciation. Olney got almost as much satisfaction out of
the renunciation as out of the fruition of his hopes. It
is apt to be so in these hypothetical cases; perhaps it
is often so in experience.

IIe waited heroically about all the next day to hear
from Mrs. Atherton. Something in the pressure of
her hand at parting had assured him that she understood everything, and that she was his friend; that
they were people of honor, who were bound to do this
thing at any cost to him, but that a just Providence
would probably not let it cost him much, or at least
not everything.

When her letter came at last, hurried forward by a
special delivery stamp that spoke volumes in itself, it
brought intelligence which at first made Olney feel
that he must somehow have been guilty of an unfair-
ness towards Bloomingdale, that he had tacitly if not
explicitly prejudiced his case. There was a little
magnanimous moment in which he could not rejoice
that Miss Aldgate had absolutely refused to see Mr.
Bloomingdale; that she had shown both surprise and
indignation at his coming; and that no entreaty or ar-
gument of Mrs. Atherton's had prevailed with her to
show him the slightest mercy, or to send him any
message but that of abrupt refusal, which Mrs. Atherton softened to him as best she could. She wrote
now that she was sure there must be some misunder-
standing, but that in Miss Aldgate's state of nervous
exaltation, it was perfectly useless to urge anything in

9

excuse of him, and she had to resign herself to the girl's decision. She coincided with Olney in his idea of Bloomingdale's character. She owned to a little fancy for him, and to a great deal of compassion. He had borne the severe treatment he received very manfully, and at the same time gently. He seemed to accept it as final, and he did not rebel against it by the slightest murmur. Olney perceived that Mrs. Atherton had been recognized as his rival's confidante far enough to be authorized to pour balm into his wounds, and that she probably had not spared the balm.

XIII.

OLNEY expected, without being able to say why exactly, a second visit from the man who was now only his former rival. Perhaps it was because he believed he knew why Miss Aldgate had refused to see him that he rather thought the young man would come to ask him. But he did not come, and in the mean time Olney began to perceive that it would have been preposterous for him to have come. Till he learned by inquiry of the clerk at the Vendome that Bloomingdale had left there with his mother and sisters, he did not feel that the minister was out of the story, and that it remained for him alone to read it to the end. He took it for granted that Rhoda treated the man who had certainly a claim upon her kindness in that brusque, not to say brutal manner, out of mere hysterical weakness. She had made up her mind to refuse him, and as she felt she might not have strength to endure the sight of the pain she must inflict, she had determined not to witness it. Whether she had loved him too well to afflict him with her secret, or not well enough to trust him with it, was what remained a question with Olney, and he turned from one point of it to the other with the wish to answer it in a sense different from both. What he wished to believe was

that she did not love the poor young fellow at all, but
this seemed to be too good to be true, and he could
not believe it with the constancy of his desire.   Never-
theless he had a fitful hold upon it, and it was this
faith, wavering and elusive as it was, that encouraged
him to think Miss Aldgate would not refuse to see
him, and that he might at any rate go down at once
to Mrs. Atherton's, and ask about her if not for her.

When he had reasoned to this conclusion, which he
reached with electrical rapidity as soon as he knew
that Bloomingdale was gone, he acted upon it.   Mrs.
Atherton received him with a cheerfulness that ig-
nored, at least in Miss Aldgate's presence, the fact
that lay hidden in their thoughts if not in hers. Olney
was not obliged to ask about her or for her; she came
down with Mrs. Atherton, as if it were entirely natural she should do so; and the pathetic confidingness
of her reception of him as an old friend, brightened
almost into the gayety that was her first and principal
charm for him.   If it had appeared at once this gayety
would have troubled him; he would have doubted it
for that levity of nature, of race, for which Mrs. Meredith had seen it; but it came out slowly like sunshine
through mist, and flattered him with the hope that he
had evoked it upon her tragic mask. At the same
time he was puzzled, if not shocked, that she seemed
forgetful of the woman, so recently gone forever, who
had been in all effects a mother to her, and who had
sacrificed and borne more than most mothers for her
sake.   He was himself too inexperienced, as yet, to

Grief is in fits or spurts

know that we grieve for the dead only by fits, by impulses; that the soul from time to time flings off with all its force, the crushing burden, which then sinks slowly back and bows it in sorrow to the earth again; that if ever grief is constant, it is madness, it is death.

Mrs. Atherton could have told him of moments when the girl was prostrated by her bereavement, and realized to their whole meaning the desolation and despair which it had left her to. But she could not have told him of the stony weight of unforgiveness at the child's heart; of her unreasoning resentment of the dead woman's revelation, as if she had created the fact that she had felt so sorely bound to impart. The tragic circumstances of her death had not won her pardon for this: the girl felt through all that her aunt had somehow *made it so ;* and for her, ignorant of it all her life till that avowal, she had indeed made it so. Whether a wiser and kinder conscience might not have found it possible to keep the secret, in which there was no guilt or responsibility for the girl, and trust the Judge of all the earth for the end, is a question which the casuist of Mrs. Meredith's school could not deal with. Duty with her could mean but one thing, and she had done her duty. Certainly she was not to be condemned for it; but neither was the affection which she had so sorely wounded to blame if it had conceived for her memory the bitter drop of hate which poisoned all Rhoda's thoughts of her. What the girl had constantly said to herself from the first was what she still said: that having kept this secret

from her all her life, it was too late for her aunt to
speak when she did speak at last. Another not involved in the consequences of her act might not have
taken this view of it; but this was the view taken of
it by the girl who felt herself its victim, and who helplessly resented it, in spite of all that had happened
since.

Whether she was in any degree excusable, or
whether she was wholly in the wrong in this feeling,
must remain for each to decide, and to each must be
left the question of how far the Puritan civilization has
carried the cult of the personal conscience into mere
dutiolatry. The daughter of an elder faith would
have simplified the affair, and perhaps shirked the responsibility proper to her, by going first with her secret
to her confessor, and then being ruled by him. Mrs.
Meredith had indeed made a confessor of her physician, after the frequent manner of our shrill-nerved
women, but even if Olney could have felt that he had
the right to counsel her on the moral side, it is doubt-
ful if she could have found the strength to submit to
him.

Olney's interest in her was mainly confined to the
episodes of the last few days, and vivid as these had
been, it could not hold him long in censure of Miss
Aldgate's behavior; he began to yield to the charm
of her presence, and in a little while hazily to wonder
what his reserves about her were. She was in the
black that seems to grow upon women in the time of
mourning, and it singularly became her. It is the

color for the South, and for Southern beauty; like
the inky shadow cast by the effulgence of tropical
skies, it is the counterpart of the glister and flash of
hair and eyes which no other hue could set off so
well. The girl's splendor dazzled him from the sable
cloud of her attire, and in Mrs. Atherton's blond
presence, which also had its sumptuousness — she was
large and handsome, and had as yet lost no grace of
her girlhood — he felt the tameness of the Northern
type. It was the elder world, the beauty of antiquity,
which appealed to him in the lustre and sparkle of
this girl; and the remote taint of her servile and savage origin gave her a kind of fascination which refuses
to let itself be put in words: it was like the grace of a
limp, the occult, indefinable lovableness of a deformity,
but transcending these by its allurement in infinite
degree, and going for the reason of its effect deep into
the mysterious places of being where the spirit and the
animal meet and part in us. When Olney followed
some turn of her head, some movement of her person,
a wave of the profoundest passion surged up in his
heart, and he knew that he loved her with all his life,
which he could make his death if it were a question of
that. The mood was of his emotional nature alone;
it sought and could have won no justification from his
moral sense, which indeed it simply submerged and
blotted out for the time.

There was no reason why he should not stay now as
long as he liked, or why he should not come again as
often as Mrs. Atherton could find pretexts for asking

him. Between them they treated the matter very
frankly. He took her advice upon the taste and upon
the wisdom of urging his suit at so strange a time;
and she decided that in the anomalous situation to
which Miss Aldgate was left, her absolute friendless-
ness and helplessness, there were more reasons for his
wooing than against it. They took Mrs. Atherton's
husband into their confidence, and availed themselves
of the daylight of a legal mind upon their problem.
He greatly assisted to clear up the coarser difficulties
by communicating as Miss Aldgate's lawyer with her
aunt's connections in St. Louis. Mrs. Meredith had
left to her niece the remnant of the property she had
inherited from her husband; and his family willingly,
almost eagerly, accepted the conditions of the will.
They waived any right to question it in any sort, and
they made no inquiries about Miss Aldgate, or her
purposes or wishes.

Olney agreed with the Athertons that their behavior was very singular, but he kept his own conjectures as to the grounds of it. They were, in fact,
hardly conjectures any more; they were convictions.
He felt sure that they knew the secret which Mrs.
Meredith believed her husband had kept from all
the world; but this did not concern him so deeply as
the belief that had constantly grown upon him since
their first meeting in Mrs. Atherton's presence, that
Rhoda knew it too. He had no reasons for his belief;
it was quite without palpable proofs; it was mere in-
tuition; and yet he was more and more sure of the
fact.

His assurance of it strengthened with his belief that the girl loved him, and had perhaps had her fancy for him from the moment they saw each other in Florence. The evidences that a woman gives of her love before it is asked are always easily resolvable into something else; and in both these things Olney's beliefs were of the same quality, and they were of the same measure. But the one conviction began to taint and poison the other. The man's sweetest and fondest hope became a pang to him, because it involved the fear that the girl might have decided to accept his love and yet keep her secret. In any case he desired her love; as before himself he did not blame her for withholding her secret till she found what seemed to her the best time for imparting it; but for her own sake he could have wished that she would heroically choose the worst. This tacit demand upon her was made from his knowledge of how safe it would be for her to tell him everything, and it left out of the account the fact that till he asked her to be his wife he had no claim upon her, that he could have no terms from her till he owned himself won. Love is a war in which there can be no preliminaries for grace; the surrender must be unconditional, before these can even be mentioned.

There were times, of course, when Olney could not believe that the girl knew what at other times she seemed to withhold from him; but at all times the conjecture had to be kept to himself. If she knew, she practised a perfect art in concealing her knowledge which made him fear for the future; and if she

did not know, then she showed an indifference to her
aunt's memory which seemed not less than unnatural.
He conceived the truth concerning her when he said
to himself that Rhoda must hold Mrs. Meredith responsible for the fact if she had imparted it; and that
time alone could clear away her confusion of mind
and enable her to be just to the means which she
confounded with the cause of her suffering. But he
could not have followed her into those fastnesses of
the more intensely personalized feminine consciousness where the girl relentlessly punished her aunt in
thought, not for doing her duty, but for doing it too
late, when she could remain through life only the un-
reconciled victim of her origin, instead of revealing it
early enough to enable her to accept it and annul it by
conforming herself to it.

As this was what Rhoda had never ceased to believe
would have been possible, her heart remained sore
with resentment in the midst of the love which she
could not help letting Olney divine. Circumstance
had drawn their lives into a sudden intimacy which
neither would or could withdraw from; they drifted
on toward the only possible conclusion together. For
the most part the sense of their love preoccupied them.
She turned from her desperate retrospect and blindly
strove to keep herself in the present, and to shun the
future as she tried to escape the past; he made sure
of nothing to build on except the fact that at least she
did not know that Mrs. Meredith had confided her
secret to him. With this certain, he could take all

chances. He could trust time to soften her heart toward the dead, and he could forgive the concealment toward himself which she used.

One thing that he could not understand was her apparent willingness to remain just where and as she was indefinitely; he did not realize that it was apparent only, and as a man he did not account for her patience — if it were patience — as an effect of the abeyance in which the whole training of women teaches them to keep themselves. The moral of their education from the moment they can be instructed in anything is passivity, and to take any positive course must be a negation almost of their being; it must cost an effort unimaginable to a man.

The summer weeks faded away into September, when one morning Olney came to see Rhoda, and found her sitting on a bench to the seaward of a group of birches. The trees had already dropped a few yellow leaves on the lawn, which looked like flowers strewn in the still vividly green grass. It was one of those pale mornings when a silvery mist blots the edge of the sea and lets the sails melt into it. She was looking wistfully out at them, across Mrs. Atherton's wall, which struggled so conscientiously to look wild and unkempt, with its nasturtiums clambering over it; but she did not affect to be startled when Olney's steps made themselves heard on the gravel-walk coming toward her.

She flushed with the same joy that thrilled in his heart, and waited for him to come near enough to

True Woman: patience Passive

take her hand before she asked, "Oh, didn't you see Mrs. Atherton?"

"She sent me word that you were here, as if that were what I wanted," he answered, smiling over the hand he held.

"Well, I can tell you myself, then," she said, sitting down again.

"Yes; or not, as you like," he returned.

"No, it is isn't whether I like or not. I am going away."

"Yes," he said quietly. "Where?"

"To — to New Orleans. To look up my mother's family." She lifted her eyes anxiously to his face, and then helplessly let her glance fall. "I have been talking it over with Mrs. Atherton, and she thinks too that I ought to try to find them."

Olney's heart gave a leap. He knew that she was hovering on the verge of a confession, which she longed to make for his sake, and that he ought not to suffer her till he had made his own confession. He had the joy of realizing her truth, and he rested nervelessly in that a moment, before he could say lightly, "I don't see why you should do that."

"Don't you think — think — that it's my duty?" she pleaded.

"Not in the least! From the experience I've had with the St. Louis branch of your family I don't think it's your duty to look *any* of them up. Why do you think it is your duty? Have they tried to find you?"

"They are very poor and humble people — the humblest," she faltered piteously. "They —"

Her breath went in silence, and he cried, "Rhoda! Don't go away! Stay! Stay with me. Or, if you must go somewhere, go back with me to Florence, where the happiness of my life began when I first knew you were in the world. I love you! I ask you to be my wife!"

She let her hand seem to sink deeper in his hold, which had somehow not released it yet; she almost pushed it in for an instant, and then she pulled it away violently. "Never!" She sprang to her feet and gasped hoarsely out, "I am a negress!"

Something in her tragedy affected Olney comically; perhaps the belief that she had often rehearsed these words as answer to his demand. He smiled. "Well, not a very black one. Besides, what of it, if I love you?"

"What of it?" she echoed. "But don't you *know*? You *mustn't!*"

The simpleness of the words made him laugh outright; these she had not rehearsed. She had dramatized his instant renunciation of her when he knew the fatal truth.

"Why not? I love you, whether I must or not!"

As tragedy the whole affair had fallen to ruin. It could be reconstructed, if at all, only upon an octave much below the operatic pitch. It must be treated in no lurid twilight gloom, but in plain, simple, matter-of-fact noonday.

"I can't let you," she began, in a vain effort to catch up some fragments of her meditated melodrama about her. "You don't understand. My grand-mother was a slave."

"The more shame to the man that called himself her master!" said Olney. "But I *do* know — I understand everything — I know everything!" He had not meant to say this. He had always imagined keeping his knowledge from her till they were married, and then in some favored moment confessing that her aunt had told him, and making her forgive her for having told him. But now, in his eagerness to spare her the story which he saw she had it on her conscience to tell him in full, the truth had escaped him.

"You know it!" she exclaimed, with a fierce recoil. "*How* do you know it?"

"Your aunt told me," he answered, hardily. He must now make the best of the worst.

"Then she was false to me with her last breath! Oh, I will never forgive her!"

"Oh, yes you will, my dear," said Olney, with the quiet which he felt to be his only hope with her. "She had to tell me, to advise with me, before she told you. I wish she had never told you, but if she had not told me, she would have defrauded me of the sweetest thing in life."

"The privilege of stooping to such a creature as I?" she demanded, bitterly.

He took her hand and kissed it, and kept it in his. "No: the right of saying that you are all the dearer to me for being just what you are, and that I'm prouder of you for it. And now, don't say that you will not forgive that poor soul, who suffered years for every hour that you have suffered from that cause. She felt herself sacredly bound to tell you."

"It was too late then," said the girl, with starting tears. "She killed me. I *can't* forgive her."

"Well, what can that matter to her? She can forgive you; and that's the great thing."

"What do you mean?" she asked, weakly trying to get her hand away.

"How came she to tell you that she hadn't told me?"

"I — I made her," faltered the girl. "I asked her if she had. I was frantic."

"Yes. You had no right to do that. Of course she had to deny it, and you made her take a new lie on her conscience when she had just escaped from one that she had carried for you all your life." Olney gave her back her hand. "Whatever you do with me, for your own sake put away all thoughts of hardness towards that poor woman."

There was a long silence. Then the girl broke into sudden tears. "I do; I will! I see it now! It was cruel, *cruel!* But I couldn't see it then; I couldn't see anything but myself; the world was filled with *me* — blotted out with me! Ah, *can* she ever forgive me? If I could only have one word with her, to say that there never was any *real* hardness in me toward her, and I didn't know what I was doing! Do you think I made her kill herself? Tell me if you do! I can bear it — I deserve to bear it!"

Substituting
a regret
for a resentment

"She never meant to kill herself," said Olney, sin‑cerely. "I feel sure of that. But she's gone, and you are here; the question's of you, not of her; and I only asked you to be just to yourself. I did'nt mean to tell you now that I knew your secret from her, but I'm not sorry I told you, if it's helped you to substitute a regret for a resentment."

"It's done that for all my life long."

"Ah, I didn't mean it to go so far as that!" said Olney, smiling.

"No matter! It's what I must bear. It's a just punishment." She rose suddenly, and put out her hand to him. "Good‑by."

"What for?" he asked. "I'm not going."

"But *I* am. I'm going away to find my mother's people, if I can — to help them and acknowledge them. I tried to talk with Mrs. Atherton about it, the other day, but I couldn't rightly, for I couldn't let her understand fully. But it's true — and be serious about it, and don't laugh at me! Oughtn't I to go down there and help them; try to educate them, and elevate them; give my life to them? Isn't it base and cowardly to desert them, and live happily apart from them, when — "

"When you might live so miserably with them?" Olney asked. "Ah, that's the kind of question that I suspect your poor aunt used to torment herself with! But if you wish me to be really serious with you about it, I will say, Yes, you would have some such duty toward them, perhaps, if you had voluntarily chosen your part with them — if you had ever *consented* to be of their kind. Then it *would* be base and cowardly to desert them ; it would be a treason of the vilest sort. But you never did that, or anything like it, and there is no more specific obligation upon you to give your life to their elevation than there is upon me. Besides, I doubt if that sort of specific devotion would do much good. The way to elevate them is to elevate *us*, to begin with. It will be an easy matter to deal with those simple-hearted folks after we've got into the right way ourselves. No, if you must give your life to the improvement of any particular race, give it to mine. Begin with *me*. You won't find me unreasonable. All that I shall ask of you are the fifteen-sixteenths or so of you that belong to my race by heredity ; and I will cheerfully consent to your giving our colored connections their one-sixteenth."

Olney broke off, and laughed at his joke, and she joined him helplessly. " Oh ! don't laugh at me ! "

" Laugh at you? I feel a great deal more like crying. If you go down there to elevate the blacks, what is to become of me? I don't really object to your going, but I want to go with you."

" What do you mean ? " she entreated, piteously.

" What I said just now. I love you, and I ask you to be my wife."

" I said I couldn't. You know why."

" But you didn't mean it, or you'd have given me some reason."

" Some reason ? "

10

"Yes. What you said was only an excuse. I can't accept it. Rhoda," he added, seriously, "I'm afraid *you* don't understand! Can't you understand that what you told me — what I knew already — didn't make the slightest difference to me, and couldn't to any man who was any sort of a man! Or yes, it does make a difference! But such a kind of difference that if I could have you other than you are by wishing it, I wouldn't — for my own selfish sake at least, I wouldn't wish it for the world. Can't you understand that?"

"No, I can't understand that. It seems to me that it must make you loathe me. Oh!" she shuddered. "You don't know how hideous they are — a whole churchful, as I saw them that night. And I'm like them!"

Olney's heart ached for her, but he could not help his laugh. "Well, you don't look it. Oh, you poor child! Why do you torment yourself?"

"I can't help it. It's burnt into me. It's branded me one of *them*. I *am* one. No, I can't escape. And the best way is to go and live among them and own it. Then perhaps I can learn to bear it, and not hate them so. But I *do* hate them. I do, I do! I can't help it, and I don't blame you for hating *me!*"

"I don't happen to hate even you," said Olney, going back to his lightness. "My trouble's another kind. Perhaps I should hate you, and hate them, if I'd come of a race of slave-holders, as you have. But my people never injured those poor creatures, and so

Branded

I don't hate them, or their infinitesimal part in you."

He found himself, whenever it came to the worst with her in this crisis, taking a tone of levity which was so little of his own volition that it seemed rather to take him. He was physician enough to flatter his patient for her good, and instinctively he treated Rhoda as if she were his patient. It did flatter her to have that side of her ancestry dwelt upon, and to be treated as the daughter of slave-holders; she who would not reconcile herself to her servile origin, listened with a kind of fascination to his tender mockery, in which she felt herself swayed by the deep undercurrent of his faithful love.

"Come, come!" he went on, and at his touch she dropped weakly back into her seat again, and let him take her hand and hold it. "I know how this fact has seized upon you and blotted everything else out of the world. But life's made up of a great deal else; and you are but one little part injured to many parts injurer. You belong incomparably more to the oppressors than to the oppressed, and what I'm afraid of is that you'll keep me in hopeless slavery as long as I live. Who would ever imagine that you were as black as you say? Who would think — "

"Ah, you've confessed it! You would be ashamed of me, if people knew! That is it!"

"If you'll answer me as I wish, I'll go up with you to the house and tell Mrs. Atherton. I've rather a fancy for seeing how she would take it. But I can't unless you'll let me share in the disgrace with you. Will you?"

"Never! It shall never be known! For *your* sake! *I* can bear it; but *you* shall not. Promise me that you'll never tell a living soul!" She caught him nervously by the arm, and clung to him. It was her sign of surrender.

He accepted it, and said: "Very well, I promise it. But only on one condition: that you believe I'm not afraid to tell it. Otherwise my self-respect will oblige me to go round shouting it to everybody. Do you promise?"

"Yes, I promise;" and now she yielded to the gayety of his mood, and a succession of flashing smiles lit up her face, in which her doom was transmuted to the happiest fortune. She kept smiling, with her hands linked through his arm and her form drawn close to him; while their talk flowed fantastically away from all her awful questions. Their love performed the effect of common-sense for them, and in its purple light they saw the every-day duties of life plain before them. They spoke frankly of the incidents of the past few days, and he told her now of his interview with the Bloomingdale family, and how he felt that he had hardened Mrs. Bloomingdale's heart against her by his unsympathetic behavior in denying them an interview with Rhoda herself.

This made her laugh, but she said, with a shudder: "I couldn't have borne to look at them. From the first moment after my aunt *told* me, I felt that I must prevent their ever seeing me again. I wrote to him, and I carried the letter out with me to post it, and make sure it went; and then somehow I forgot to post it."

"Ah," said Olney, "I suppose that's the reason why he came to see me, and to ask where he could find you."

"Yes," answered Rhoda, placidly.

"There is only one thing in the whole affair that really troubles me," said Olney, "and that's the very short shrift you gave that poor fellow."

"Why, when I had written to him I would not see him again, I supposed he was persisting, and it was only the other day that I found the letter, which I'd forgotten to post. It was in the pocket of the dress I wore that night to the church."

"And you don't think his persisting — his caring so much for you — gave him the right to see you?"

"Not the least."

"Ah, a man never understands a woman's position on that question."

"Why, of course, if I had cared for *him* — "

"I don't know but I've a little case of conscience here myself. I had awful qualms when that poor fellow was talking with me. I perceived that he was as magnanimous as I was on the subject of heredity, and that, I thought, ought to count in his favor. Will you let it?"

"No."

"Why not?"

" Because I don't care for him."

" How simple it is ! Well, he's off my conscience, at any rate."

She began to grieve a little.   " But if you are sorry — "

" Sorry ? "

" If you think you will ever regret — if you're not sure that you'll never be troubled by — by — *that*, then we had better — "

" My dear child," said Olney, " I'm going to leave all the trouble of that to you.   I assure you that from this on I shall never think of it.   I am going to provide for your future, and let you look after your past."

She dropped her head with a sob upon his shoulder, and as he gathered her in his arms he felt as if he had literally rescued her from her own thoughts of herself.

He was young and strong, and he believed that he would always be able to make her trust him against them, because now in the fulness of their happiness he prevailed.

There are few men who, when the struggle of life is mainly over, do not wonder at the risks they took in the days of their youth and strength ; and it could not be pretended that Olney found more than the common share of happiness in the lot he chose ; but then it could be said honestly enough that he did not consider either life or love valuable for the happiness they could yield.   They were enough in themselves. He was not a seeker after happiness, and when he saw that even his love failed at times to make life happy for his wife, he pitied her, and he did not blame her. He knew that in her hours of despondency there was that war between her temperament and her character which is the fruitful cause of misery in the world, where all strains are now so crossed and intertangled that there is no definite and unbroken direction any more in any of us. In her, the confusion was only a little greater than in most others, and if Olney ever had any regret it was that the sunny-natured antetypes of her mother's race had not endowed her with more of the heaven-born cheerfulness with which it meets contumely and injustice. His struggle was with that hypochondria of the soul into which the Puritanism of her father's race had sickened in her, and which so often seems to satisfy its crazy claim upon conscience by enforcing some aimless act of self-sacrifice. The silence in which they lived concerning her origin weighed upon her sometimes with the sense of a guilty deceit, and it was her remorse for this that he had to reason her out of. The question whether it ought not to be told to each of their acquaintance who became a friend had always to be solved anew, especially if the acquaintance was an American; but as yet their secret remains their own. They are settled at Rome, after a brief experiment of a narrower field of practice at Florence; and the most fanciful of Olney's compatriot patients does not dream that his wife ought to suffer shame from her. She is thought to look so very Italian that you

would really take her for an Italian, and he represents
to her that it would not be the ancestral color, which
is much the same in other races, but the ancestral
condition which their American friends would despise
if they knew of it; that this is a quality of the despite
in which hard work is held all the world over, and has
always followed the children of the man who earns
his bread with his hands, especially if he earns other
people's bread too.

W. D. HOWELLS.

CRITICISM AND FICTION. With Portrait. 16mo, Cloth, Ornamental, $1 00.

Mr. Howells is charming. One finds no end of pleasure reading these light, bright, piquant pages. Many a good thing and many a true thing is here clothed in the diction of a master.—*Independent*, N.Y.

A BOY'S TOWN. Described for HARPER'S YOUNG PEOPLE. Illustrated. Post 8vo, Cloth, Ornamental, $1 25.

In no novel of his are we more fascinated from cover to cover than in this truthful narration of a boy's life.—*Hartford Courant*.

THE SHADOW OF A DREAM. A Story. 12mo, Cloth, $1 00; Paper, 50 cents.

A tale full of delicate genius, in the front rank among its kind.— *N. Y. Sun*.

A HAZARD OF NEW FORTUNES. 12mo, Cloth, 2 vols., $2 00; Paper, Illustrated, $1 00.

Never has Mr. Howells written more brilliantly, more clearly, more grimly, or more attractively than in this instance.—*N. Y. Tribune*.

ANNIE KILBURN. 12mo, Cloth, $1 50; Paper, 75 cents.

It certainly seems to us the very best book that Mr. Howells has written.—*Spectator*, London.

APRIL HOPES. 12mo, Cloth, $1 50; Paper, 75 cents.

A delightfully humorous and penetrating study of Boston society.— *Boston Transcript*.

MODERN ITALIAN POETS. Essays and Versions. With Portraits. 12mo, Half Cloth, $2 00.

Mr. Howells has in this work enabled the general public to obtain a knowledge of modern Italian poetry which they could have acquired in no other way.—*N. Y. Tribune*.

THE MOUSE-TRAP, AND OTHER FARCES. Illustrated. 12mo, Cloth, $1 00.

PUBLISHED BY HARPER & BROTHERS, NEW YORK.

☞ *The above works will be sent by mail, postage prepaid, to any part of the United States, Canada, or Mexico, on receipt of the price.*

BEN-HUR: A TALE OF THE CHRIST.

By LEW. WALLACE. New Edition from New Electrotype Plates. pp. 560. 16mo, Cloth, $1 50; Half Calf, $3 00.

Anything so startling, new, and distinctive as the leading feature of this romance does not often appear in works of fiction. . . . Some of Mr. Wallace's writing is remarkable for its pathetic eloquence. The scenes described in the New Testament are re-written with the power and skill of an accomplished master of style.—*N. Y. Times.*

Its real basis is a description of the life of the Jews and Romans at the beginning of the Christian era, and this is both forcible and brilliant. . . . We are carried through a surprising variety of scenes; we witness a sea-fight, a chariot-race, the internal economy of a Roman galley, domestic interiors at Antioch, at Jerusalem, and among the tribes of the desert; palaces, prisons, the haunts of dissipated Roman youth, the houses of pious families of Israel. There is plenty of exciting incident; everything is animated, vivid, and glowing.—*N. Y. Tribune.*

From the opening of the volume to the very close the reader's interest will be kept at the highest pitch, and the novel will be pronounced by all one of the greatest novels of the day.—*Boston Post.*

It is full of poetic beauty, as though born of an Eastern sage, and there is sufficient of Oriental customs, geography, nomenclature, etc., to greatly strengthen the semblance.—*Boston Commonwealth.*

"Ben-Hur" is interesting, and its characterization is fine and strong. Meanwhile it evinces careful study of the period in which the scene is laid, and will help those who read it with reasonable attention to realize the nature and conditions of Hebrew life in Jerusalem and Roman life at Antioch at the time of our Saviour's advent.—*Examiner,* N. Y.

It is really Scripture history of Christ's time, clothed gracefully and delicately in the flowing and loose drapery of modern fiction. . . . Few late works of fiction excel it in genuine ability and interest.—*N. Y. Graphic.*

One of the most remarkable and delightful books. It is as real and warm as life itself, and as attractive as the grandest and most heroic chapters of history.—*Indianapolis Journal.*

The book is one of unquestionable power, and will be read with unwonted interest by many readers who are weary of the conventional novel and romance.—*Boston Journal.*

PUBLISHED BY HARPER & BROTHERS, NEW YORK.

☞ *The above work sent by mail, postage prepaid, to any part of the United States or Canada, on receipt of the price.*

By CONSTANCE F. WOOLSON.

EAST ANGELS. pp. 592. 16mo, Cloth, $1 25.

ANNE. Illustrated. pp. 540. 16mo, Cloth, $1 25.

FOR THE MAJOR. pp. 208. 16mo, Cloth, $1 00.

CASTLE NOWHERE. pp. 386. 16mo, Cloth, $1 00
(*A New Edition.*)

RODMAN THE KEEPER. Southern Sketches. pp.
340. 16mo, Cloth, $1 00. (*A New Edition.*)

There is a certain bright cheerfulness in Miss Woolson's writing
which invests all her characters with lovable qualities.—*Jewish Advocate*, N. Y.

Miss Woolson is among our few successful writers of interesting
magazine stories, and her skill and power are perceptible in the delineation of her heroines no less than in the suggestive pictures of
local life.—*Jewish Messenger*, N. Y.

Constance Fenimore Woolson may easily become the novelist
laureate.—*Boston Globe.*

Miss Woolson has a graceful fancy, a ready wit, a polished style, and
conspicuous dramatic power; while her skill in the development of a
story is very remarkable.—*London Life.*

Miss Woolson never once follows the beaten track of the orthodox
novelist, but strikes a new and richly loaded vein, which so far is all
her own; and thus we feel, on reading one of her works, a fresh sensation, and we put down the book with a sigh to think our pleasant
task of reading it is finished. The author's lines must have fallen to
her in very pleasant places; or she has, perhaps, within herself the
wealth of womanly love and tenderness she pours so freely into all
she writes. Such books as hers do much to elevate the moral tone of
the day—a quality sadly wanting in novels of the time —*Whitehall
Review*, London.

Published by HARPER & BROTHERS, New York.

☞ *The above works sent by mail, postage prepaid, to any part of the
United States or Canada, on receipt of the price.*

BY MARY E. WILKINS.

A NEW ENGLAND NUN, and Other Stories. 16mo, Cloth, Ornamental, $1 25.

A HUMBLE ROMANCE, and Other Stories. 16mo, Cloth, Extra, $1 25.

Only an artistic hand could have written these stories, and they will make delightful reading.—*Evangelist*, N. Y.

The simplicity, purity, and quaintness of these stories set them apart in a niche of distinction where they have no rivals.—*Literary World*, Boston.

The reader who buys this book and reads it will find treble his money's worth in every one of the delightful stories.—*Chicago Journal.*

Miss Wilkins is a writer who has a gift for the rare art of creating the short story which shall be a character study and a bit of graphic picturing in one ; and all who enjoy the bright and fascinating short story will welcome this volume.—*Boston Traveller.*

The author has the unusual gift of writing a short story which is complete in itself, having a real *beginning*, a *middle*, and an *end*. The volume is an excellent one.—*Observer*, N. Y.

A gallery of striking studies in the humblest quarters of American country life. No one has dealt with this kind of life better than Miss Wilkins. Nowhere are there to be found such faithful, delicately drawn, sympathetic, tenderly humorous pictures.—*N. Y. Tribune.*

The charm of Miss Wilkins's stories is in her intimate acquaintance and comprehension of humble life, and the sweet human interest she feels and makes her readers partake of, in the simple, common, homely people she draws.—*Springfield Republican.*

There is no attempt at fine writing or structural effect, but the tender treatment of the sympathies, emotions, and passions of no very extraordinary people gives to these little stories a pathos and human feeling quite their own.—*N. Y. Commercial Advertiser.*

The author has given us studies from real life which must be the result of a lifetime of patient, sympathetic observation. . . . No one has done the same kind of work so lovingly and so well.—*Christian Register*, Boston.

PUBLISHED BY HARPER & BROTHERS, NEW YORK.

☞ *The above works sent by mail, postage prepaid, to any part of the United States, Canada, or Mexico, on receipt of the price.*

SEVEN DREAMERS.

A Collection of Seven Stories. By Annie Trumbull
Slosson. pp. 286. Post 8vo, Cloth, Ornamental,
$1 25.

A charming collection of character sketches and stories
—humorous, pathetic, and romantic—of New England
country life. The volume includes "How Faith Came
and Went," "Botany Bay," "Aunt Randy," "Fishin'
Jimmy," "Butterneggs," "Deacon Pheby's Selfish Nat-
ur'," and " A Speakin' Ghost."

They are of the best sort of " dialect " stories, full of humor
and quaint conceits. Gathered in a volume, with a frontispiece
which is a wonderful character sketch, they make one of the
best contributions to the light literature of this season.—*Observer, N. Y.*

Stories told with much skill, tenderness, and kindliness, so
much so that the reader is drawn powerfully towards the poor
subjects of them, and soon learns to join the author in looking
behind their peculiarities and recognizing special spiritual gifts
in them.—*N. Y. Tribune.*

These stories are of such originality, abounding in deep pathos and tenderness, that one finds himself in perfect accord
with the writer as he reads of the hallucinations of these he-
roes.—*Watchman, Boston.*

Dreamers of a singular kind, they affect us like the inhabitants of allegories—a walk of literary art in which we have had
no master since the pen dropped from the faint and feeble fingers of Hawthorne, and which seems native to Mrs. Slosson.—
N. Y. Mail and Express.

The sweetness, the spiciness, the aromatic taste of the forest
has crept into these tales.—*Philadelphia Ledger.*

Published by HARPER & BROTHERS, New York.

☞ *The above work will be sent by mail, postage prepaid, to any part
of the United States, Canada, or Mexico, on receipt of the price.*

CHARLES DUDLEY WARNER.

AS WE WERE SAYING. With Portrait, and Illustrated by H.W. McVickar and Others. 16mo, Cloth, Ornamental, $1 00.

So dainty and delightsome a little book may it be everybody's good hap to possess.—*Evangelist*, N. Y.

OUR ITALY. Illustrated. 8vo, Cloth, Ornamental, Uncut Edges and Gilt Top, $2 50.

In this book are a little history, a little property, a few fascinating statistics, many interesting facts, much practical suggestion, and abundant humor and charm.—*Evangelist*, N. Y.

A LITTLE JOURNEY IN THE WORLD. A Novel. Post 8vo, Half Leather, $1 50.

The vigor and vividness of the tale and its sustained interest are not its only or its chief merits. It is a study of American life of to-day, possessed with shrewd insight and fidelity.—George William Curtis.

A powerful picture of that phase of modern life in which unscrupulously acquired capital is the chief agent.—*Boston Post.*

STUDIES IN THE SOUTH AND WEST, with Comments on Canada. Post 8vo, Half Leather, $1 75.

Perhaps the most accurate and graphic account of these portions of the country that has appeared, taken all in all. . . . A book most charming—a book that no American can fail to enjoy, appreciate, and highly prize.—*Boston Traveller*.

THEIR PILGRIMAGE. Richly Illustrated by C. S. Reinhart. Post 8vo, Half Leather, $2 00.

Mr. Warner's pen-pictures of the characters typical of each resort, of the manner of life followed at each, of the humor and absurdities peculiar to Saratoga, or Newport, or Bar Harbor, as the case may be, are as good-natured as they are clever. The satire, when there is any, is of the mildest, and the general tone is that of one glad to look on the brightest side of the cheerful, pleasure-seeking world with which he mingles.—*Christian Union*, N. Y.

PUBLISHED BY HARPER & BROTHERS, NEW YORK.

☞ *The above works will be sent by mail, postage prepaid, to any part of the United States, Canada, or Mexico, on receipt of the price.*

LaVergne, TN USA
07 January 2011
211499LV00003B/111-114/A

9 781594 621529